E. Luminata

By Diamela Eltit

D1452071

Translated by Ronald Christ

With the collaboration of
Gene Bell-Villada, Helen Lane and Catalina Parra

a la amidstad de Ronald Christ

Lumen, Inc.
40 Camino Cielo
Santa Fe, New Mexico 87501

©1997 Lumen, Inc.
ISBN: 0-930829-40-9
Printed in the United States of America
Originally published as *Lumpérica* ©1983 Diamela Eltit

Excerpts from *E. Luminata* appeared previously, slightly different, in *Grand Street* and SITES Architecture.

Translation, Afterword © Ronald Christ 1997
Photograph of Diamela Eltit © Lotty Rosenfeld 1980

ERRANT, ERRATIC

This preface brings me to a crossroads where I must come to grips with certain elements that, apparently, reoccur in my books as well as with social conditions of the time in which it has been my lot to write. Therefore I will try to re-read some of my preoccupations over these past years. But, I want to point out that whatever I may say is relative: it must be detached, it seems to me, from the novels I have written, because these books respond to a creative activity with its own laws, from which I myself am absent and, beyond that, for which I feel totally unresponsible most of the time. Just as I feel that I could not re-write one single page of a book I have already published, I think that my writing contains questions within a space that exceeds me. And maybe that is what keeps alive my desire to write: that voice which gets away from me and which, many times, exalts or shames me.

I should add that even as I am holding to a line of thought and possibly of writing, my certainties are being mobilized as I proceed, and that is why I try to avoid, whenever possible, any kind of authorial pronouncements. I avoid them because I feel that if this kind of thinking has any meaning it is as a personal process that allows me to establish changes and modifications that are always necessary — but not necessary for shaping discourse that ends up by ideologizing itself, by paralyzing itself and halting a mental journey that I find truly important to keep under way.

I shall speak then, loosely, partially, about a few subjects.

WRITING UNDER DICTATORSHIP
The really hard thing was living under dictatorship. Living under dictatorship is inexpressible, part of a story that to me seems interminable. I cannot expand on this subject as I might like, but writing and thinking in the midst of that situation was a form of self-rescue. The condition is something so delicate, in some ways so unnarratable, that I am hard pressed to refer to it without falling into commonplaces. How can one define the effects of negative, sordid, prying power? Learning to coexist with powerlessness; putting up with a state of daily humiliations, which can be felt deeply when one is a public

4

employee under dictatorship; struggling not to find solace in indifference; surviving in the midst of a hopeless, helpless economic emergency, among other situations — that was my way of living for many, too many years.

I lived in a territory where history mingled with hysteria, crime coupled with sales. The signs of negative power fell mercilessly on Chilean bodies, producing disappearances, illegalities, indignities. I wrote in that environment, almost, you could say, obsessively, not because I believed that what I was doing contributed materially to anything at all, but because it was the only way I could save — to put it somehow — my own honor. When my freedom — I don't mean *freedom* in the literal sense but in its whole symbolic range — was threatened, then I took the liberty of writing freely. Of course, for those who published during that period, the atmosphere did not favor anything uncontrolled in regard to culture. But no it did not, nor is that the center of the conflict. Publishing under dictatorship was, without doubt, desolate. But, in my case, on account of the kind of work I do, I will always carry with me a place that is quite small. And that's fine. I think that anyone who publishes a book expects the culture to respond receptively; the fact is, in 1986 I realized that I had passed unscathed through an ordeal by fire when my novel *Por la patria* was launched to widespread critical indifference.

I wrote four books under dictatorship, and social space is what I recovered for myself during that period. But never for an instant did that make up for the wrongs, the humiliations, the fear, the suffering or the powerlessness of the system's victims. Writing in that space was something passional and personal. My secret political resistance. When one lives in a world that is collapsing, constructing a book perhaps may be one of the few survival tactics.

The military dictatorship produced a violent cut in the circuits of cultural and literary communication, and my literary development, most especially my development as a writer, took place during those years of the military regime. But I also ought to say, as a positive recollection from those years, that I had the privilege of maintaining an important dialogue with writers and visual artists — such as Raúl Zurita, Nelly Richard, Lotty Rosenfeld, Carlos Leppe, Eugenio Dittborn, Carlos Altamirano, Eugenia Brito (to recall some names from the early years) — and that dialogue permitted me an important exercise of thought when, as a group, we posed for ourselves a series of questions that provoked various attempts at answers. Among these questions perhaps the most important was the recurrent one of a possible relation, the real distance, between art and politics, between art and society. Each of these individuals — I think — is still trying to find an answer, and I hope to keep this question alive in myself.

MARGINALITY

The truth is that when I wrote this novel, beginning in 1976-77, I fixed myself entirely along one axis of feeling. I can't say that I chose this axis, at least not consciously, in so far as there was no alternative for me. And later, when the book was published, I had to read its signs of marginality for myself. I then grasped that in each of my books a thread appears and reappears in the forms of spaces, characters, or feelings that might be connected by aspects relating to certain marginalities. I have worked in various ways with beggars in shelters, with prostitutes. These people fascinate me, because they are excluded. I believe that they are a potentially powerful force to the degree that they are negatives, photographically speaking, of society. In them you see everything that people do not want to see, the blights of society. What's more they have their own beauty, happiness, liberty: a prostitute is an ordinary, everyday woman, with her joys and sufferings; a vagabond is a human being who has lots of goods: more than just one house, he has the whole city as his home.

But, perhaps most significant for me is that in appealing to instances of marginality I have been able to organize some structures of meaning. And I think that what may be understood by marginality, what has marked my own marginality as a writer, may really be grounded in structure. The word and its centering or decentering, its aesthetic consonance, its play and its mockery and torsion, constitute the greatest challenge that I must face in the process of writing. The splendid activity concentrated in the telling of stories — that's not in my line of aspiration and so, it remains outside the focus of my interests. For me, it is more important to take shelter in every possible ambiguity bestowed by the habit of writing with words and, from there, to emit a few meanings.

Nor do I see my work as experimental; rather, it is an exploration of proposals for change or innovation within certain linguistic procedures found in traditional literary craft. I am participating, dialoguing if you like, with an amplification of certain perceptions and certain literary procedures, but this is no experiment. An experiment may turn out or not; what I make is a work.

What interests me in writing novels is the artisanry — I mean: a word, another word, that exact unique word, the page —; the slowness with which meanings become organized; a certain notion of time (while I write my own life is annulled, my own death suspended); the interconnected and paradoxical stages of creation and death that come into play; the confrontation at every moment of the sense and senselessness of a craft so ambiguous and, on the other hand, so material . . . anyway.

All this is to say that I write only because I like to, because I have a passion for writing; and if I like to write, then I will write what I like. And that is why my only limitations are my own limitations, which, clearly, unfortunately, are varied and constant.

As a novel, *E. Luminata* a undertakes to force a breach in novelistic form, it is a way of making an assault on the genre as a monolithic, linear mode of storytelling. Up to this point I have not considered writing a monolithic novel based on the logic of its mechanisms; just the opposite, what has interested me have been deviations permitted by fragmentation, plurality, the edge and the border. I believe that Juan Carlos Lértora says it better than I when he speaks about what he calls "dispersion." Dispersion is what always defines the margin because it calls into question the centers and their unity. I keep to the edge of insinuation. Working with bits of materials, scraps of voices, exploring vaguely (I mean to say, like a vagabond) genres, masquerades, simulacra and verbalized emotion — that has been my literary place. The truth is that I appreciate those places, but that doesn't mean I think they are the only possibilities in literature; on the contrary, I feel that literature is truly multiple and that what matters is to construct certain aesthetic spaces that convey meanings. I believe that here lies the heart of the literary dilemma.

OTHER MARGINS

On the other hand, I have resigned myself to the idea that I have the mind I have and no other, that I have only the syntax I have. My scene of aesthetic and social unrest — I must recognize this — is set in elusive areas, certain places where power or regulation (or whatever it's called) tends to settle accounts that in the end always turn out to be unfavorable, detrimental. I take my example from what I have observed of the dominant codes that are — to say it one way or another — Chilean. I refer to those behaviors that appear to me exclusive or reductive, those that, from their anachronistic basis in class or in their economic voracity, devise determinants of conduct that, when not stereotypical, are repressive.

But behind all this lies one of the few convictions that governs me, and that is my awareness of belonging to a country with multiple social difficulties, a country marked by inequality. Perhaps it is on account of these inequalities, which are experienced by Chilean men and women and which by now have become vices, that I set down the sole act of political rebellion possible for me: rebelling socially by putting on paper writing that is somehow refractory to comfort, to comfortable signs. Perhaps I have been wrong in everything I have said up to now, and what's more it seems that the overheated and commercial direction of these times contradicts me; but I continue to think of literature as disjunction rather than as a zone of answers that leave readers happy and contented. To my way of thinking, literature, more than being an entertainment, is a generator of conflict. It ought to be serious work for the reader. I refuse to accept that literature can be consumed as though it were chewing gum or that it requires less effort than watching one of those movies that make the rounds in video cassettes. The part of me that writes is neither comfortable nor resigned and does not want readers who are not partners in dialogue, accomplices in a certain disconformity. The (ideal) reader to whom I aspire is more problematic, with gaps, doubts — a reader crossed by uncertainties. And there the margin, all the multiple margins possible, mark, among other things: pleasure and happiness, but disturbance and crisis as well.

Since I was not born with a silver spoon in my mouth and each day take on the salvaging of my family's subsistence as well as my own, I am continually made to toe the line of women who work, and I carry that discipline within me but also the legitimate and legal rebelliousness of the socially subordinated woman. Maybe that is why, after a childhood in a poor neighborhood, hurt by family circumstances, as daughter to my father and his hardships, I am open to reading the symptoms of neglect, whether social or mental. My greatest political solidarity — unrestricted, epic even — is with those spaces of neglect, and my aspiration is to a greater social stability and to flexibility in the power structure.

BEING A WOMAN,
BEING A WOMAN WRITER IN CHILE

I think that writing is a social instrument and cannot be sexualized. Its practice in history, its *mise-en-scène* — to say it somehow — has mostly been the domain of men, but that is information. Significant perhaps, but only information. Thus to me it seems reductive to conduct, on the basis of biological sexuality, the bi-polar criticism of reading works linearly as feminine-women, masculine-men. Instead, my interest lies in how bodies come to have their shape, but bodies of writing, with relative independence from the author's sex. At present I think the conflict rests on determinants of gender. And here it becomes evident that what is assigned to the masculine gender moves specifically by administration of the central powers; in contrast, what is understood to be feminine is what remains subordinated, peripheral to those powers. I know that what I'm stating may seem simplistic — perhaps it is —; but I am very clear about this being a subject of greater complexity, and I do not consider myself a specialist: I only try to think/to think about it for myself, from my own poor, particular trenches.

In this context, for example, operations created according to novelistic norms interest me. There are women writers who are masculine — it's a metaphor — in their manner of working with codes, and there are writers, on the other hand, who decenter the centers (like Joyce) and place themselves nearer the category of the feminine. I don't mean as sexual identity, but in the sphere of social conventions, such as the convention of gender. And of course there are all the intermediate points, limits, fluctuations. I want to point this out because it is obvious to me that one may play with the construction of determined bodies of writing, loading them with signs, and for me it is a matter of strategy which body of writing is formed, which sign emitted. I say the same about the wish to read literary themes as the sole symptom of a work's filiation. For example, a novel that tackles the theme of political nonconformity within a conservative literary canon may not result in criticism, precisely to the degree that its means of production remain untouched. Or a novel that presents itself as feminist or feminine or by a woman will not be transgressive merely by virtue of its referentiality to problems of reality. Therefore my idea always is to read the texts and to find their political points within them.

In any case, I believe that the political *mise-en-scène* of every artistic work is consonant with the administration of its materials, according to the meanings it irradiates. Writing novels is not an innocent activity: deploying linguistic materials sets out a political meaning, a politics of writing. And investigating that political pattern, the passage through words in order to interrogate the signs of a crisis, is what interests me. I think I understand that certain feminist theory and criticism seeks to clarify actions taken in crisis or by way of resistance, or the subject's quality in some writings by women. And that is important. But there is another critical modality that endorses any woman's literary work with a sociological reading. This reasoning does not persuade me, since on its basis women writers might come to inhabit a vast ghetto, in a better periphery, where they would compete among themselves while the central system remains un-touched.

Nevertheless, in spite of everything I have said, there is another factor: the social and cultural space where the woman writer's struggle takes place. Her concrete life as a writer. And here lies a great problem. I don't want to speak for anyone but myself because that wouldn't be appropriate. What I am going to point out — for me it has no larger significance in relation to my work — I want to state here only as a didactic exercise. In my own personal case, I have experienced the effects of discrimination, concealed within various expressions. The "hard to understand," which, when applied to some men writers perhaps might be a prestigious badge, a challenge to reading, in my case has ended up being a deter-ministic, excluding label. The act of trying to maintain a cultural discourse centered on problems that writing presents has given me the paradoxically bad reputation of being

perceived as "very intellectual". And by no means is that "very
intellectual" a compliment; rather, a way of dismissing one
channel of communication. But, after all is said and done, this
constitutes one rule in a particular cultural game. I do not
think there is explicit bad faith in such attitudes; I read in them
only how women's speech and actions are unconsciously
called into question. Apparently it is hoped that women will
respond to certain dominant models in which their word, their
writing has issued. Many of these models seem very fragile to
me because they have been so simplified as to be stripped of
nuance. The space of true-romance magazines is not the only
possible space for women, neither is that of unlimited abnega-
tion nor of anecdotal sexual freedom. More important, it
seems to me, is displaying the pondered constellation of a
thought that connects the individual with the public, the
subjective with the social.

In what has been called "triple labor," I battle as an
employee who depends on her monthly salary, as head of my
household, as a writer. There are many roles and doublings
here. And none of it's easy. And since it is not easy, my great
challenge is to make these responsibilities compatible — so
far as one can — and to make my time for writing productive.
For the rest, all the hobbles attending the woman who writes
cannot be attributed to the external world, nor to men in
particular. Many of the obstacles are even in woman's psyche,
the effects of judgments by the culture in which she was born.
I have questions myself, though they seem tricky to me, that
form part of the conventions with which I grew up, and I think
that they will be with me until I die. I believe I understand, in
part, the culture I live in, its successes and failures. Women are
not the only minority confronting diverse powers: there are
ethnic, sexual, economic minorities with similar conflicts.
Although I feel committed to each of the symbolic and civic
struggles to improve the situation of women, I have neither the
power nor the capacity to change national habits, nor would I
like to convert myself into a fiery preacher who must correct
public or private actions. Making literature is, I believe, a
revolutionary activity: comparable to that of certain household
appliances which rotate their gears in order to shake up their
own contents. In the face of so many ironic or malign or unjust
particulars that hem in the woman who writes, all I want to do
is to establish a field of questions and then to use them to

formulate an accusation. All I can do is to write my books freely, without falling into any program — either indulgent or redemptive — and to fight for their publication. What more could I do. I write because I like to. Truth to tell, I am only one writer, a woman writer, among many others.

Diamela Eltit
Santiago de Chile

1.1   The remains of this evening will be a feast for E. Luminata, that woman who recrosses her own face, incessantly appliquéd, though no longer shining brightly as in time past when viewed under natural light.

That's why the electric light makes her up by splitting her angles, those outer edges at which she jostles toward the cables that carry the light to her, languishing her right up to the finishing touches to her whole body: but her face in bits and pieces. Anyone can testify to her half-open lips and her legs stretched out on the grass — crossing or opening — rhythmic against the backlight.

In which the nightfall sustains the square in its decoration, so that she may strike her own fleeting poses which derive her as far as exhaustion, turned on by the advertisement that falls in light upon the center of the square, amid trees and benches, till she reaches the pavement where she remains with her back turned.

Because the cold in this public square is the hour appointed for assuming a proper name, bestowed by the signboard that will turn on and off, rhythmic and ritual, in the process that will definitively give them life: their civic identity.

The ragged people of Santiago arrive, pale and stinking, in search of their space: the name and alias that like a token will guarantee them a trip, but one calculated in terms of their previous expenditure of flesh until they are shod with light from the neon sign.

And so they will be generically named the pale people as a provisional ranking. The ones who come from the most distant points toward the square which lit up by electrical networks guarantees a fiction in the city.

And so here they are and their countless poses: the cables are their point of view in the gaze's parallel of pleasure. She waits anxiously for the illuminated sign and that's why when she feels touched she stirs all over, with her breast heaving and her eye moist. The lighted sign does not stop. He goes on printing out the sum of names that will confirm their existence; this

pencil of light spread over the center of the square that in
literature produces lists, in the chill of dawn, while the other
pale people take refuge against the trees in a grouping made
almost beautiful by the sharpness of their silhouettes.

E. Luminata in the center of the square starts to convulse
again. The pale people rotate their heads to get a better angle
and only then do they fan out across the lawn. Attentive, they
rivet their gaze on the baptism, while the illuminated sign
directly strikes her who, frenetic, moves her hips under
the light: her thighs rise from the ground and her drooping
head pounds from so much striking against the pavement.

It confirms her name in two parallel colors, that lighted sign
spread across her body writes E. Luminata and runs rhythmi-
cally through the possible gamut of aliases: it writes her
fugitive and the letter falls like a take in a film. Yet, with so
complex a name that she takes up the gibberish again and
that's why the sign's message assumes a classic role that
becomes medieval in its constancy, in the orthodoxy of its
form, in the frigidity of its construction.

Not in vain do they approach the center just as she withdraws
and right there they display the bodies that posit no differences
between some of them and the others: the illuminated advertisement coats them with various shades, tints them and
conditions them.

They moan for light, orgiastic in their convulsions they clump
together. Who would think that in Santiago de Chile there
could be this baptized one, just so those people might swell
like buds. But that's how it is, with branches of trees licking
the faces and her rubbing up against their wood from sheer
pleasure in the spectacle. Plunged into the ecstasy of shedding
her personal scab so as to be reborn hairless in the company of
people who, like commercial products, are going to be put on
offer in this desolate citizenship.

That's how she might have been in spite of the cold: exposed
horizontally after losing her proper name, immersed, seeking
the light with her eyes popping from the transparency. More
pale people in their sallow skin wringing out the pleasure at

any cost, gazing at each other in the square, with razed heads, transported by electricity, stammering.

They, who could have shone some other way, are here licking the square like goods of uncertain value.

In literature they might be compared to sapphires, opals, celestial aquamarines.

To say it again:
Light from the neon sign, which is installed atop the building, falls into the square. It's a lunatic plan for covering the pale people of Santiago who have clustered around E. Luminata merely as a visual complement to her forms.

Because this sign that lights up at night is constructing his message for them, who reach their full complement only at this hour when they follow their predictable paths.

Like criminal assaults in their threatening presences.

That's why the illuminated sign, wholly autonomous, calls them by literary names; for example, the sign was saying/ Sandalwood, but the impulse died as it fell over their skin bristling up in such a highly speculative metamorphosis.

The sign was saying Peltasgiant kite. The sign was saying/ crucible.

She shattered the impulse to paint those lips the sign's writing had made for her.

That's why in the square two kinds of electrical systems are coupled: one allotted to the quadrangle, the other sliding down from the illuminated sign — that light that sells itself. So in counterpoint her lips have lost their submissiveness and her figure once again becomes deceptive beneath the rays that converge in the center. But she is not alone there. All her possible identities have sprouted wildly — pinning down her anatomical points — overshooting her beyond her areas. Ruled only by a schedule assigned to the electric light in shaping the illuminated message that striates her.

The pale people have taken possession of the square's corners and huddle their bodies there shielded one against another, their rubbed-against bodies that during the baptism exchanged aliases through their starving pores.

They touch each other and pawed over they yield.

Names upon names with their legs intertwined they draw close in translations, in fragments of words, in jumbles of letters, in sounds, in movie titles. Words are written on their bodies. Convulsions with fingernails across flesh: desire opens furrows.

That's how the corners of the square become activated by packed bodies that, one on top of the other, lead to an exterior. But not in their penetration, in their appearance rather, in remaking a name for themselves, they exude delight and reappropriated constitute the scene.

The pale people's flesh reveals in their openings their process and on merging into the next one following they mark off infinite possibilities for any gaze. They fall into and out of their ranks, forming a deceptive boundary for the square.

But the neon sign supports them. It continues its twinkling with precise regularity. E. Luminata in the center. She is sweating despite the cold and that's why her flesh is exposed to the luminosity. More than ever she sparkles there controlling her chiaroscuro with contortions, while the light strikes the benches in the square, the trees, and the fabricated layout of the lawn.

She slides down onto the grass in order to wallow about and cool her flesh.

This uneven lawn lets patches of earth show through, so grass and soil stick to her skin. For the one gazing at her she is a spectacle laid waste because she stammers. Each one of her names is belied by what a sight she is.

But she shines, even in depths of darkness she shines.
As the baptized one she celebrates herself in their midst, while

her own hands caress her intimately, disappearing amid her hollows. Starting from the worst vulgarity in order to reach extreme delicacy by means of poses.

She lets scraps of language be heard, remnants of signs. Undermined by dirt and grass. Nourished by sap.

She observes herself, as if her name bestowed other traits on her. She touches her skin at the same moment that she bends even farther over the grass, until her head falls onto the softened ground.

Posing repose.

Still, she keeps an eye on the illuminated advertisement, her face slightly contorted with rejoicing at the twinkling, while she slides her tongue over her lips, the wet tongue that moistens them.

Her legs are open in a negligent pose and she shifts them each time the center of the square receives the light.

The pale people have now come into that same center and they start their own show. They crowd their bodies together and let them fall onto the cement. That's how they move in a rhythm so difficult to visualize that only the illuminated sign keeps them in order when it shows their clowning.

With guttural sounds they fill the space in a virginal alphabet-ization that alters the norms of experience. And that's how from conquered into conquerors they are transformed, standing out in their swarthy tones, their flesh acquiring a true dimension of beauty. Because even she could be compromised by the chance arrangement of bodies. The same ones being readied for a new cycle.

Though that's nothing new: the sign announces bodies for sale.

That's right, bodies are sold in the square.

Not at a fixed price. It's more the pleasure they emanate from the depth of their commitment. Their words fall into the emptiness, amplifying their molecules in order to petrify the production's everlastingness.

Why bother saying that they call her when they structure their voices in the space.

They turn into heartrending sound.

It could be — perhaps — from the virility of its massiveness the Beloved who on summoning her lays siege in order to possess her, this vagrant who lies stretched out in the square, arousing with her indecent movements who knows what dreams of surrender.

But those pale people stay in the center rubbing themselves against the concrete, rolling under the wooden benches, thinly dressed despite the cold: always moaning.

But it's already been said that what escapes from their lips aren't exactly moans.

An untrained ear might hear in their individualities a heart-breaking spectacle. But that's not it. It's the salvation of she who is baptized.

Their identities are being celebrated. They are their own godparents who are being received and she, she's the one who is rechristened in each one of them.

It's a feast.

The illuminated message continues falling, giving them more possibilities, extending their stock of imagery.

They are seen projected to the limits of Santiago, decked out in finery: by thefts and excesses gaining entrance everywhere. Proprietors out of sheer desire as they sell themselves to the sign like merchandise. These are the ones who wait eagerly.

That's why they melt with joy when they can glimpse their possibilities amid sheaves of light from the illuminated sign.

The deal's done already and that's why the happiness of those bodies impresses gracefulness on their movements.

Harmony has settled into the square.

Neither does E. Luminata stay out of the show. She has emptied her mind of all memory and now constructs and plans only with those pale people as a referent: molded into her future.

She, staged by the observation of her movements, struts erect toward the center of the square in order to stop beneath the light from the sign that illuminates her intermittently. That's how she does her first film shot:

> She's there in the middle of the square, as her feet slip from under her. The ragged people's seething bodies that, with neon lighting effects falling from a nearby building, producing on their skin a slightly distorting, phantasmagoric tint.

> It might be maybe an orgiastic shot what with the heaping up of so much flesh, but, instead the framing shows only the baptized one's purity. The scene's rhythm also incorporates an intrinsic eroticism for the shaping power of the gaze.

> The lumpen until the moment when she stands stockstill remains rigid, in a forced, hard-to-hold pose, so that their faces may show the difficulty of the work, the self-denial of their concentration: their true beauty in the tenseness of their features.

> A long take lasting three minutes in which two cameras are used to get the necessary speed.

> It's evident, in wide angle, that the scene is a public square. The lampposts, the benches, the trees, the grass and some neighboring structures are visible. The frame is cropped just at the point where the sign sheds its light, at the top of the building.

Then they get up off the ground with their flesh bristling from the cold and walk toward the corner in order to dress up with calm gestures, and their limpid faces can be seen among the lights.

REMARKS ON THE FIRST SCENE
The scene shows only the constructing of a pose with the lumpen and E. Luminata, their bodies facing the camera in an experimental work, managing in the space of three minutes to aesthetically compose an admiring gaze at themselves. A gaze mediated by the camera that besieges them and under which, by two-dimensional lighting effects, they submit and are submitted in front of the others in the triumphs of their beauty.

NOTES FOR THE FIRST SCENE
To cinematically compose something like a mural in the public square, highlighting what's marginal in the spectacle. That way turning back the canons of identity across the lump sum of bodies which neutralize individual features to the utmost, so as to produce collectively an image purged of those who, being cut out, have limbered their substance by consciously submitting to desire.

In short, the offertory.

So:

> Unspectacular withered skins.
> Pleasure reflected in their faces.
> In spite of the lighting keep it a night scene.
> Grant autonomy and flexibility to each one within his pose.
> Continuance of the grouping.
> The ecstasy of the extra who recognizes himself on the screen as a structural element.
> Point out the defect in the gaze, the fictiveness of its angle.

Dwell on those same withered/ wasted faces, those same faces which posed against the night, that man will have seen as his peril when they emerge, taking him by surprise at the corners. And that man then — sweating — will press his legs together because his penetration instead of rejoicing will be white soot.

Maybe that's why terror will hasten that human figure's steps toward forgetting such an image.

Because that one, he intuits the ulcerated legs and whose hands, as the night advances, lower trousers to re-examine one by one the open sores that no longer respond to any treatment/ bandaged with filthy rags to avoid friction against the cloth covering them and that's why, on feeling them next to his healthy skin, those same suppurating legs will again stain his cleanliness, the incessant care that anyone lavishes on himself.

But finally, on screen, terror and desire for his own whiteness and hygiene will reveal themselves as errata and then he will let his footsteps take him to the public square, he will raise his eyes to the illuminated sign, he will unburden himself of clothes, he will spread his legs stretched out on his back on the concrete, and out of desires he will have consummated himself in another, until that same concrete, in the painfulness of the pose, breaks his skin and then that one will see himself in each of his sores and decorated his skin may shine with light from the illuminated sign and only that way may he truly know some kind of life.

Ah, the public square from wretched to sublime. Delirious, that's what it is.

Because the square produces aberrant ramblings.

For example:
If the pale people who obtained a new civil name dispensed with E. Luminata they would lose their support, that's to say, maybe no one would proclaim this act.

It's she who will transmit the news, her face transformed like a preacher's, its multiple facets, that absolute lack of inscription will indicate the truth of the event.

But it's not time yet: she just barely constructs herself in each one of them. They still haven't pulled themselves together yet and once again they look at the proofs. As a group they have made their corrections, their repairs, cleansing themselves of their remains of miseries and imperfections.

MISTAKES IN THE FIRST TAKE

The tense bodies were rigid, not from inner necessity, but from effects of the camera: such as terror.

She did not show her best angle herself, sneaked a look directly into the camera, turned her face during the zoom. The snipping of her hair was too regular, the expected tears did not well up, her eyes scarcely grew moist. She looked more defiant than calm, moved her lips several times. She avoided rubbing against the pale people.

That's why she is resting in the square. Everyone agrees how hard the work is. They are stretched out on the grass watching the blinking of the sign that prints itself brightly on the ground. The electric light grows stronger denoting the green of the grass, the benches, the trees.

Cars circle by with their headlights turned on. Noises fill the square.

They know that in a few hours they will have to come to terms with the next stage. They prepare for it by excising each one of their bodily particles. Now indeed, they are certain beyond a shadow of a doubt that the mistake will not be repeated.

1.2   That's why the remains of this new nightfall will be the true meeting of E. Luminata and the pale people who, lost in their wandering by chance, will arrive in the square to stretch out full length on the benches, but with insomnia visible in their pupils.

Their eyes that retain the impress of everyday places: their endless walking through the streets with their gaze always scanning every interior that opens itself to them, so as to preserve those images they will review in precise detail when they reach the quadrangle at the hour when the lights go on.

Of course they stretch out on the benches and she looks at them, astonished at the homogeneity of the sight. Her muscles tense as she finds a place for herself at one corner to get a better vantage point. It can be deduced without erring that her overall state is precarious, her breathing troubled, that gleam in her eyes.

Her hands reach out, she grasps the nearest tree and brings her face toward it: that face wet with tears, until she draws it away from the bark and then one of her decisions in the square emerges:
        She smashes her head against the tree.
She smshes her head against the tree again and again until the blood overflows the skin, it bathes her face that blood, she cleans her face with her hands, looks at her hands, licks them. She moves toward the center of the square with her forehead wounded — her thoughts — she parades her pleasure in her own wound, she probes it with her fingernails and if there is pain it is obvious that her state leads to ecstasy.

        She exhibits herself waiting for the fall of the sign upon her wound.
        Yes, I had a wound myself, but today I have and drag my own scar. I no longer remember how much or what way I suffered, but from the scar I know I did suffer.

In the square she says — I'm thirsty — as she feeds on herself, on her surplus, and her stained clothes take fire from the fall of the sign. She hugs herself, licks her hands again and still moist with saliva her hands rub her arms. She writhes in spasms at the peak of her energy. The pale people sit erect on the seats and in each one of them dawns compassion, she repeats:

— I'm thirsty — and her lips smile.

She dries her face on the hem of her dress that gets stained, the blood still clouding her gaze. She turns toward them and looks them over with her personal stamp. Her wound is open and the degree of injury is still not apparent. She raises her hands and fully conscious guides her fingers to her face in order to further part the open skin. Her gaze is blank and there in the middle of the square, only for the pale people, she lets out a howl and her piercing voice expands and extends into the darkness.

Her cry surprises them and those ragged people rise to their feet and little by little begin to approach her. They surround her so as to gaze at her up close. But they do not touch her, their eyes also moist/ from compassion their eyes.

— but I myself certainly saw that one's eyes misting over and falling upon me so as to cover me with his passionate hands, the same ones that solicitous cured my wounds. His hands —

Even though they know she requires precisely that space in order to put on her show. She has assumed another identity: did it through literature.

That way she recognizes herself in her own image, the one reflected on the ground when a new pencil of light falls from the luminous sign. That's why thirst undermines her and her tongue repeats its movements over her lips.

She stretches out on the pavement in order to extract the freezing cold. Her breathing grows regular and the pale people also tell their bodies apart and remain in the middle of the square still shaken by the echoes of the cry.

It has been said that their eyes are fixed on other landscapes, but she, in the depths of her pose, is beginning to blot out that image; with her wounded face she is the one who unquestionably rules them.

Her face of glass beads, her skin like diamonds.

Unquestionably it's for them that she prepares herself to take on the possibility of redoing the baptized one. Primal, she makes herself present absent protection, by her own will power she is ready for the control of the illuminated sign which, in the dark, achieves his deep penetration. Everything is ready, she smoothes her clothes, raises her face: a void has been produced in the square.

But the illuminated sign does not stop. It goes on transmitting proper names until the square is reduced to her and the pale people who with a fixed gaze recognize themselves in the flashing.

They await their turn, for the illuminated sign to confirm them as existence, that is, name them another way: they are reborn that way in this purifying passage, less impallored now, because it blots out their color, confirming the voluntary loss of their civil records. That's why in the square that encloses them they prowl in the direction of the light, restoring them to an ancient happiness. Incubated anew, they get life from technology.

Where outside the square could they obtain that privilege?

The pale people, with heads raised, turn toward the illumi-nated sign and start their hip movements, perceptible even under their clothes: their thighs touch and they rise from the ground. They can see them adopting other identities mani-fested in anatomical death rattles.

Over the body they pass, first the name and then its whole gamut of aliases.

While those others continue their mimetic manipulations near the grass up to the point of burying their heads between their knees.

The transfixed by insomnia, the stereotyped by paleness, the dazzlers.

Synthesizing in their singular name all the others cast down by the illuminated sign to the point of gathering unto themselves the identity based on their diverse appearances. And that's why, she is the first to show up in that quadrangle, when visibility is low, when eyes can mistake their object.

The illuminated sign goes on hurling down names and aliases, crossing over them, and that way nobody will be razed, nobody will let tears fall upon skin; those limp and abject from nausea on the concavity.

Those who have received their own names by birthright can never know anything about the daze from being so lost in different residues that only the climax of paleness remains as an alternative, as mere disposable flesh.

They see the experimentation in the square, not solitary or sought after: forced, that's what/ she plots her pose and holds it for a lapse of life.

That's how she once more detaches her old crusty scab.

Having abandoned herself to the illuminated sign's rhythm of switches, and squarely facing each stroke, she clutches her head, dragging herself toward the concrete bench, her face wasted from the movements that drive her toward the edge.

— she was still trembling for those seconds so as not to move in segments because she was parted from plenitude while receiving, jinxed, such proofs of scorn, not measured in hours when raised up and exhausted she stretched out in translucent pores —

— she was not jam-packed to overflowing between the legs so as to receive the illuminated sign against her breast all night long, until her back was the vein of the trees that received her at each battering, laid waste/ she was an image. Her legs flared up with apprehensions produced on command from her brain. Each surname was constituted in sculptured simpleness/ vetoed her rhythm in a coded discourse, versifying —

— she pressed up against the tree trunk to leave there the sign that rubbed in now demolished her cornea until she lost consciousness —

— she had no other face that could be exchanged higher up as merchandise —

Her cry still resounds in the square, growing shriller with the sign's falling only to resume with the same intensity as when first emitted. Her cry that becomes circular until the pale people cover their ears to regain the normality of the square. They converge on the center, fleeing the sounds. They approach her so that she will command cut; she who confronting that reproduction redoes her own delirium. Her mouth opens at each interspace. She copies with her mouth, dubs herself/ the trees, the lawn, the cables, the lamps, even the benches are pierced: a new sequence has been produced.

SECOND SCENE, PRODUCTION OF THE CRY:

Lumpen take places on the benches that surround the axis of the square. She stands upright exactly in the middle. From the nearby building the sign lets his intermittencies fall, clarifying her image. Darkness spreads around there. Cameras roll.

The camera captures her from the moment when slowly she stretches herself out face down on the ground to hold that pose for a few seconds. They set up an overhead shot, showing the form of lumpen curled up on benches, focusing on her figure stretched out on the ground.

Simultaneously, the other camera follows her in a close-up of her face touching the ground, lips slightly parted until she raises her head, holding it erect for a few seconds and violently smashes it against the ground, striking the area of her forehead which cracks open releasing the blood that will instantly bathe her. She will sit on the ground with her head between her knees and remain that way for a few moments. She will get up and when touched by the sign from her mouth will burst the cry. The pale people will sit straight up in their seats. They will be recorded in overhead shots. They will remain motionless nearby. And then the cry will be produced again and again.

The scene will be cut on the shot of the sign up to her entering the building.

So that she may sit on a bench in the square and there only her mouth murmur — I'm thirsty — that spent face, the deep circles under her eyes/

Ah, for a mere glance, for a gesture, I would have told another story.

REMARKS ON THE SECOND SCENE:
Engender by means of the wound what's required for producing a cry. Same doesn't lead immediately to the wound, but only some seconds later; it's not exactly an automatic cry of pain, but rather an instance useful for justifying the wound. To put it differently: it's not the wound that causes the cry, but precisely the reverse: for her to be wounded the cry was necessary, all the rest's pretext.

That's why the continuing repetition of same. Returning to it continually amplifying it up to earsplitting so that it's gradually transformed — by technology — from the feminine timbre to differing masculine cries but preserving the same inflections: identical curves in range.

Until finally they begin to superimpose cry upon cry as well as to annex her voice in extreme distortion. Besides mixing in a minor key other sounds — for example — citizens who abruptly come to a halt. In the image lumpen present traces of placidity — why not say it, of happiness really.

NOTES FOR THE SECOND SCENE:
Immediately after the wound has been produced bring up the sound's dominance by means of the image's static quality. It will be filmed only in medium shots and overhead takes. The

sequence's power is the cry which will be in contrast to the facial detachment. The relative indifference. That's how she, the one newly baptized will revert to the primal howl.

And so:
     The collectivized baptismal ceremony.
     Because he who is freed from sin emanates.
     Bathed in liquid/
     Lifted up.
     The ragged people who receive the sign's rays.
     In order to be repeated on screen like documents: the
          baptismal certificate.
     The outcry from the redeemed one.
     So that her shrieks deafen those same extras.
     They will be like fever and obscenity.
     Until tight in the throat they cease.

That's why the pale people will stretch out on the benches in the square, hoarse from the effort, overwhelmed by their rasping, getting themselves ready for the stages that the sign procures for them, offering them the sum of literary names crossed by traditions that convert them on short term into decorative merchandise.

They accede to the cry that will save them. In order once again to become objects of desire, up to the limits of manipulation. When they will be multiple, colorful, written anew and marked, losing themselves in who knows maybe what habitable spaces through dreams of this territory.

Through literature it will be, so that cry may be linked up again and even the illuminated sign will bend letting his sheaf fall upon her body, the transparency. And then grown green exit the square and the square will be the single nonfiction in this whole invention.

Because the baptized, she also leads to wantonness. See them in the ceremony with their pale faces and the features in which they offer themselves like the ruined woman who sells herself — at any price — just so they'll accept her in her profession: as this E. Luminata who only on offers herself to the gaze, who sells herself to her image.

For example:
If her directorial voice did not demolish the square then the production of the cry would be cut off outside. That's why on the basis of the event she originates the possibility of also producing in the others' throats the same course of her fusion.

That way she'll allow the expansion until the square — then — is nothing but a cord stretched to its tautest along which those tones, high pitched or low, converge in different channels, and through outcry draws nigh the purification.

MISTAKES IN THE SECOND TAKE:
No doubt about it they've gotten better this time. These same people have taken off like professionals, let their bodies go, submitted to the admiration conditioning their looks. In short, they have learned from the performance.

Still, there stands in the way the unconditional decorum of their voices, this perpetual prissiness. Those who back out aseptic in the screaming just don't make it. If this cry doesn't pierce, it's no good. It would have to be stepped up in the studio, by mixing voices, electronically.

But that's not how it will be.

The mistake in the cry, its reserve, will be redone in the same square until they open themselves up and she is filmed at her peak. She, who by the bruiting of her voice, solely in order to be projected on screen, is capable of effectively dubbing the baptismal cry.

Solely for that the cry goes on repeating in the square and becomes coherent with the winking of the illuminated sign. That way at each of its falls the cry rises up as an accompaniment.

Cry and illuminated sign stalk each other/

Like enemies in the night they compete.

Until the coming together becomes inevitable and spills out of the square itself in the obscene embrace where cry and sign couple. They merge into one another and finally — in the dead of night — the sacrament spurts forth as one.

The sacrament in the square, the rubbing out of the past and these same beings — the city's lumpen — writhe in convulsions so as to immerse themselves in its center, to be touched on the pate bending down to the concrete, supplicants, with saliva dripping down and eyes reddened by the dazzling light. These same ragged people who raise their hands to their breasts and gently feel their heartbeats.

Because they are not armies in the night, they are nothing really. Or rather the setting in motion of the baptized one's primal moment, when natural water is replaced by technology which more effectively penetrates and bedazzles.

Their eyes open, their pupils dilate at such a wonder and every movement, every garment will show the two faces of the sacrament. Because to be reborn is to extract the moment of the fall, the vice that they were laying down and to leave it is the ultimate sacrifice so that the square — as a considerate place — will suck into itself their depravities and boiled over be the place of memory, when lost and desperate they would drag their heads across the grass before the illuminated sign gave them life.

That's why the square is lit at night. Only for that.

Whose hands turn on the electric light? Who are the benches in the night for?

But she is surrounded by lumpen who run through their parts, their assigned roles and the motionlessness that drives them to boredom. These are the takes, the mere exhibition of their bodies that become bothersome from being so much theirs. That's why they search themselves to get the benefit that is their due. They rummage through their cinematic memory and it is the absence of color, except for the night's, the lack.

Because there are no colors, traces of tints yes.

Though that's not exactly right, the existing tonalities create no surprise because of their everyday status.

That's the problem.

But they save it just when they will have to rest in what remains of this night. They will go toward the benches, not to sleep, but to reimpress on their pupils images.

Saved and redone they will stay.

1.3   Still in the nighttime — in the dark — they come
back to the square and that's why:

1.   The pale people come back to the square to remain
       there with bodies swollen, backs leaning against the
       trees.

       trees — lawn — electric light — concrete
       branches and cables that carry light to the lampposts
       lampposts that also illuminate the benches
       and my madonna face looking into her madonna face.

2.   The pale people remain in that position despite the
       cold that cuts across their face and makes them hide
       their features.

       they turn them differently — cover them too —
       ragged people, pale people
       I'm thirsty (in the square) I'm freezing (in the square)
       silhouetted brow — lips — nose — entirely silhou-
       etted by electric light
       and my madonna face seeks her madonna mouth and
       inside touches her profane tongue.

3.   Because remaining all that time exposed to the cold
       and rigidity makes the body stiff as a board.
       scattered like statues — intensely pale — in the
       square
       knees trembling — ears aching — lungs gasping for
       air
       hands afflicted — face frozen — body weary
       and my madonna tongue moistens her tremulous
       madonna tongue.

4.   The square is no place for darkness. Each time the
       electric light divulges their bodies leaning against
       the trees.

       at an appointed hour — when it grows dark — public
       lighting comes on
       all the lamps shine brightly in the square
       the electric light falls upon the square lit up along its

edges
and my madonna tongue touches her madonna breast
and moistens it.

5.   Can it be an hallucination in the square? Can those
        bodies be branches? Let's rub out such auguries.

        mental monody in the square — of forgetfulness —
        of ecstasy
        of ecstasy and malice — of sadness — of madness
        of many errors — of mind gone blank — of work
        and my madonna lips suck her madonna breast
        longingly.

6.   What if their skulls were open? And if there were
        probes and bandages?

        don't beg anymore — with that look — nobody
        believes you
        pale people take pleasure, rusty from light on their
        heads
        crooked skulls — razed heads — sodomites —
        vulgar
        and my madonna mind entreats her madonna mind
        and touches it.

7.   And what if they were losing blood? And if the blood
        drained out of their bodies?

        I'm thirsty (in the square) — they pant — sit down
        — lean against the trees
        smashed heads — scalpels along the edges — metal
        bands
        the needle enters — pierces the flesh — the indi-
        vidual falls asleep
        and my madonna furrow seeks her infertile madonna
        furrow.

8.   What if all this were an error? And if they were
        nothing but a fistful of lost souls?

        search for pale people in Santiago — dark souls —

sallow figures
sterilized operating rooms — pregnant odors —
motor noises
surgical flasks — translucent gauze — open wounds
and my madonna hand touches her hot madonna
knees.

9.   And what if they were sentenced for crimes? And if
        they were only dragging their sentences?

        it is no longer turned on — no longer glows —
        the electric light
        they are far away — they are spread out — the cables
        they no longer lean on each other — they no longer
        shelter each other — amid the trees
        and my madonna knees clamp her madonna knees
        tightly.

10.   All the same no: they stay on in the square in the
        midst of this cold with their spines stiffened.

        their features stigmata — marked by fire — scorned
        transparent skin — withered faces — diluted gazes
        beneath the Chilean sky — benches of stone and
        wood
        and my madonna hands spread her madonna knees
        and they lick her.

1.4   When at nightfall the sleepless arrive decked out at the chosen place. Now that the cold increases and the body turns lapis. Such cold in the square that lungs are flooded and even breathing is difficult.

Actually, the darkness becomes difficult to conceal. Even the bulbs turned on by the city do not absorb the gloom and the benches in the square would seem to be wet with frost.

That's why they will have no rest. Only for moments at a time can they let themselves fall steadied against a tree in order to resume any kind of activity and that way work off the stiffness.

They appear wrapped up in strange garb. Every fashion is announced in tatters, but the color always subdued, faded.

The same opaqueness that's also complemented by their faces.

Rather a pile of rags envelops them: they are bundled up in garment upon garment.

Because spending a night outdoors in this cold requires resolute preparation and that's why they also resort to accessories of newspapers, branches, refuse: anything that in burning might warm them.

They are standing at one of the square's corners. They rub their hands together and shuffle their feet. From their mouths, the steam of their breath escapes. Their faces are silhouettes half blotted out by the backlighting.

But the illuminated sign gains in these conditions. Falling upon the center of the square spills the sign even farther into the pitch dark. Nothing obstructs its glow, that's why they look at it from time to time and these people are still moved by its increasing brightness.

And she herself, who has taken her place, makes her way slowly toward the sign's image and plants herself beneath in order to be imprinted.

Her gray garments receive the sign's shades, serve as a screen for its projection.

Because a dress of thick gray wool covers her. On her, scarcely functional clothing, but nevertheless it particularizes her. Her practically razed head shines under the sign's lights and cannot avoid the moving that warms her.

They are pierced by the cold that in Santiago, under the open sky, becomes unbearable.

Their faces drawn by this effect. She trembles and then they start piling up their trash: they will light a fire. No surprise to the one watching them, because the night is teeming with these people, warming themselves at any cost.

It's true that they have lighted a small fire to one side of the square's center. The farthermost edges of the figure constructed by the illuminated sign are diluted, though in an overall view preserving its features. They draw closer to it; even E. Luminata, who was watching them from a distance, withdraws from the center of the pencil of light to join the group of pale people.

They constantly feed the fire and gaze hypnotized into the flames which, though weak, warm them.

They stretch out their hands and bring their faces closer, some of them throw on more branches and papers to keep the fire going. Finally they sit down around it. She remains standing though her hands are raised over the flames too. She raises her hands to her face and rubs herself with them.

All sound from outside the square has ceased; even the cars have stopped going by, that's why any movement they make becomes apparent. Nothing obstructs them.

She has stepped back a few feet from the group, persists in turning to the illuminated sign. She raises her head to the light, but immediately begins moving her feet. Those others are still fascinated by the fire, their hands remain outstretched and in their faces can be seen a hint of color. Some cough from the smoke, but they build up the fire again. The hardness of the ground forces them to change positions and some even stand up, though they do not move from the spot.

In the midst of her swaying back and forth she looks at them and on her face appears a special grimace. She observes them attentively as she hugs her own body and rubs herself with her hands. From her angle can be seen the clustering of bodies, the outlined silhouette of their outstretched arms, the profiles of those faces. Looking at them she smiles with an indulgent, even admiring expression.

She also determines that the fire is on the verge of going out. She herself begins to walk around the square and in spite of the darkness she succeeds in making out papers or branches or cardboard boxes. All this she begins gathering up in her arms. She goes toward those others and lets the meager fuel fall. She goes back to the corners of the square and here and there collects its trash.

Time passes. She returns on the last trip, but from her hands fall some few papers and a branch or two.

And so, she has now cleaned the square.

But the blaze will still be fed for another lapse of time. They will be protected from the cold, so that she can go on observing them by the light from the sign and that way examine the perfection of their poses and each hand extended over the fire may be analyzed in its particularity, as well as their curved backs, their movements and even the sound of their clothing.

That's why she changes places in the center of the square. She moves down this center line as a point of view until she brings into sight which face belonged to which back, in order to see the other outstretched hands, the profiles, the expression that accompanies the change in pose. That's why her gaze is steady and her face eager. Now the cold doesn't matter, she would forfeit pleasure in the viewing if she merged with one of them and for that same reason nobody would bear witness to the scene: adjusting the angles, gauging the growth of the fire each time it is set up.

She changes positions so rapidly that the dizzying view allows only the observation of fragments. Like a traveling shot her gaze. But the other gaze will also be widened and she will be recorded there as the one who looks.

Because if this image they have created is one of sadness, it is also one of pleasure.

Because the sign arranges them in a changed order of magnitude.

Although the warmth of the electricity is inadequate it produces aberrant ramblings. That's why she prefers it and the pale people draw close enough to its rubbing to set themselves ablaze.

But let's go back. If the flames keep them warm they owe that to her. But not as kindness, it's been for her own delight. For the visions she gets out of their grouping.

At last she's had enough of looking. She now begins to follow the shades that the neon sign leaves on her clothing. A beam marks her clothes and leaves her iridescent. Differently from the flames' light on the pale people's silhouettes, as though technology embellished her while leaving the others in the ghostly tradition.

Those others appear opaque and reduced; she in contrast is constructed.

It seems impossible for them to remain quiet next to the fire. They begin frequently turning their faces toward the one who places herself under the illuminated sign and one by one they get up in order to draw near.

They have not concluded the ceremony.

They have left her a space so she can approach the fire without their bodies rubbing against hers. She projects her own features through the flames, framed by the illuminated sign that embellishes her.

She takes her place.

Lumpen arrange themselves among the lights in the square.

She is hypnotic looking into the reddened flame: the heat
makes her drowsy, her eyes close half way, her body curves
seated on the ground, her overall posture is one of repose.

But oh how they defy her: that way of stopping under the
lights so as to provoke her: another identity taints them.

So that she will respond they goad her with unmistakable
signs, sap her strength, encourage her to push herself to the
limit.

She has lowered her eyes so as not to look at them. She resists,
entreats, for the first time, the illuminated sign. The fire has
lost its innocence.

She checks her impulses and her teeth bite into her lips, her
hands pressed together. She sweats.

From insolent gestures they proceed to indifference, but
there's no denying that they harass her, and on top of that the
sign's dizzying rush, the whole square turns menacing.

Only so that she will murmur — I'm thirsty — drawn close to
the fire, defenseless, tyrannized by her own stay — when
stunned myself I too have felt beside myself knowing what
was in store for me, solitary and inflamed (I was burning hot)
and this stricken face offered me just one alternative —

Only so she that she will be granted a new identity does she
resort to tradition and like a quotation, facing the fire she
brings her hand near, stretches her hand out over the flames
and lets it fall upon them.

Satisfied they stretch out under the lights, rest their heads on
the concrete. They do not look at her.

And her hand open over the flames changes color, her face
also turns red. She looks at her hand, the blisters that are

rising, the contraction of the fingers.

The new injury has been produced and because of it other injured make their appearance. A new circuit has been opened in literature.

She rests her hand on the cold concrete. Shivers. Convulsions are upon her.

She says — I'm thirsty — and the others now start to watch her without missing one of her movements. Aliases fall upon them appropriately. Now there are no traces of protest: Go forth baptized.

Terror fills her — she no longer feels pain — or perhaps she feels it but that unfocused gaze brings her to losing her balance. She does not see her hand which she has moved away from herself in order to leave it on the concrete, her hand fallen onto the ground.

Because for all that remains of the night she will not go near them. Her night of glory that propels her from despair to this happiness, to the one stretched out on the square's cold concrete. And now it's not only she, but also the theft from the others.

And so the burned one will give her a new scar that will forge her body as she wills.

She has burned her hand in the incipient pyre and her black-ened flesh shrivels the skin. She exposes her arm confirming the difference in color. She is absolutely out of pain now. And for the first time she looks at them and now it is she who is provocative. Not one cry has escaped her lips. She is a professional.

She looks at them and for them raises her hand. The fire is dead and only the reflection from the sign and the lamps allow her gesture to be observed. She spreads her fingers slowly. Shows the palm of her hand. Covers her face with it.

That's how they will remain molded so that stiff and chilled they may be erected into victimizers as their assigned role, in order once again in this performance to become the victimizers of their own defenselessness. With this new power they swell still further. The night has granted them autonomy.

With the palm of her hand between her lips she says — I'm thirsty — and it is her own lips that hurt it with their movements.

But then with her mouth stuck to her hand she broaches the opposite meaning of her phrase. She deconstructs the phrase word by word, syllable by syllable, letter by letter, by sounds.

Twisting its phonetics. Altering the modulation she converts it into a foreign tongue. It is no longer recognizable and with difficulty her strained throat emits the signs. She takes her hand from the mouth deprived of the message's legibility. That's why her open mouth is no longer capable of producing sound, let alone words.

She has disorganized language.

Her efforts are considerable. She seems more like a mute who in her need for expression gesticulates, opening her mouth exaggeratedly, half closing her eyes and then is changed into a grotesque spectacle for him who, effortlessly, and in harmony can be heard.

She looks sick.

One of those limited in their abilities who insist on appearing before the healthy in order to join in with them.

The ragged people in the center of the square are surprised and compassion fills them. Their bodies very close, without any beating about the bush they are touching each other. It's something more than a means of protection. They trace the outlines of their solid bodies under the luminous sign. Gazing at her in that state of deterioration, having pushed her to that by the diminished value of their gaze makes them succeed in constituting themselves as others.

Clustered in the center and pawing each other while that woman continues to rebel against her condition.

For the time being, out of sheer cruelty, the next sequence is set up.

THIRD SCENE:

She is filmed from the moment she approaches the fire.

A traveling camera until she stands at the edge of the small fire.

With cutting the scene will show the slow gathering of the pale people under the lights. It will be a medium shot. The camera will return to her as she lets herself drowse beside the fire in a relaxed pose, a posture that takes into account the agreeable warmth until she slowly turns her head toward the lumpen. Then the camera takes them and shows the intensity of their gazes, the general longing, a perverse body language rather. The camera takes her in her resistance. She tries to shut her eyes so as not to see them. She can't. Finally she turns toward the flames and very slowly stretches out her left hand in order to plunge it in. Her head sinks on her breast and only the angle of incline is perceptible.

In close-up the camera captures her hand being consumed in the flames until she withdraws it. Now it takes the lumpen who no longer watch her, absorbed as they are in the sign's rays.

She lets herself fall upon the pavement and moves her arm away from her body until her hand rests on the ground. The part of her face that modulates — I'm thirsty — is shot in close-up and the camera pulls back and shoots the square in wide angle.

A take three minutes long.

Because someone might say that nobody would burn her own hand for a mere look/ oh if you say that it's because you know nothing about life.

REMARKS ON THE THIRD SCENE:
In this scene four moments converge that are not independent of each other:

The illuminated sign that is going to rule this new identity, the pale people who acquire it, she who submits, as well as burn and word as one.

That's why gaping grimace, gestures, expressions are in the process of being developed. The subtlety confirms this scene at an extreme limit in view of which the transfer ought to be total. That's why the interchange in the situation should be exploited. What's presented here is a scene based on the power of seduction that each of the elements exerts over the others.

It's to be seen as that, a dramatization of the one seduced. From her resistance up to total surrender. That same humility of surrender in those who, torn, are astonished at their successes. That's why the indifference, the modesty, the passion, the terror of those who film and are filmed come to the surface and that's how the one who brings her hand so close to the flames as to scorch it is the same one who by conquering is conquered.

This scene is about surrender.

This power of the gaze, its dazzling force.

NOTES FOR THE THIRD SCENE:
It will be constructed with extreme delicacy. That's the only way they will face the camera humbler than in time past. They will be stripped of any defective bad habits. That's why they will be made completely malleable when before their very eyes the change is brought about. Surprise at its fragility will spur them on to perfection.

Every subtlety is considered here so the camera, which will be specially managed, will make its appearance and travel, as though made of gauze, like some fragile material it will be guided. In the same way the illuminated sign, the benches, the trees, the cables, the lamps, the lawn will imprint themselves on the screen with equal discretion and distance.

That's why:
> When fingers from the cold stiffen.
> Breathing slows down the pain in the back being
> sharp
> the body's bones ache
> and all the coats are not enough
> tears run down the face from the cold
> and that alone is why she cleans the square until the
> frost confuses her and her hand remains exposed
> to the flame she has tended herself and out of
> indifference falls into the fire.

She overflows herself into what pain leaves like a hole and she, the confused one surrenders there. From sheer willpower another structure is erected and she, she is the sum of the others who are resplendent in aggression.

And may every word then be identical to the corporeal flash upon being reformed in another space with the square as backdrop. The evocation of this constructed landscape; the city's breathing space.

Light from the sign, wound, cry and attack — let them be converted into just an echo of the lumpen who undergo transformations until their skin turns phosphorescent and the image of literature tackles and conditions a few writings. Embodied in the gleam wrested from those withered hides, cheapened. Because stretched out in the square their minds will become bodies so that E. Luminata — as matter for observation — may knock to bits the nightmare of these nights in letters.

If for example:

The illuminated sign had not fallen upon the center of the square they would not have assented to the baptized's privilege. Literature is constructed from chances, from the hypothetical arrival in the square of some few who seat themselves on the benches so that others will look at them and decipher them. And what's sold by irradiation from the sign installed atop the nearby building is equal to the surplus value someone could take from a few words spread out across the book.

The book displaying the illuminated sign that sells: language, that's what it will be.

And she who at great pains arrives in the night with a price put paid roams from sign into symbol, until beside herself she is one of those cases it would be better to forget.

The above said, seal it and stumble it. Shut down the scene. Burn the takes. Detest the camera.

MISTAKES IN THE THIRD SEQUENCE:
Out of exhaustion more than anything else certain disparities have arisen. A few not paying attention haven't come into the take at precisely the right moments and even, the light falling from the sign appears as opacity. They're tired, even she who toed the line has let her hand fall upon the flames rapidly, without feeling, in an indifferent gesture. Often in this take she has looked at them disdainfully remarking their features, as though she sought other horizons.

They weren't looking at her, because her getting burned did not move them and she herself seemed to be picking up trash in the square just to pass time, that's to say, to be doing something during her stay.

But nonetheless, these same people have succeeded, in spite of everything in showing their most pritheeing looks. They have shattered a couple of prejudices. They know they're essential for their good behavior.

Although truly they have gone through it again: gesture by

gesture, step by step headed out of the camera's range and in this repetition they have dragged their hands across the cold concrete in the square, snaked across it like animals and in their dragging along they have confirmed the absolute lack of any foundation. That's why like the deranged they seek her and lick her body, embrace the pavement, reach the lawn. They have done the scene over and then she has not plunged her hand into the fire, but, calm and peaceful, has said — I'm thirsty — and with helping hands lumpen have provided her with relief and she has gone touching them one by one, like a blind woman who wanted to retain the other's features, their possible expressions. All have been touched and each one of them has provided heat for her.

Because the cold certainly was real: it cut across the bones, plucked out the soul. And stiff as boards they have known themselves during these hours beyond all sickness: they have stayed like cradled babes.

They knew always that the scene would be done over, nobody desires such sufferings for herself.

Because out of kindness they also remain and their performances are still more precise, highly technical, because in each scene the injury is prevented.

Let's see her with her hand held out in the square. It's one of the most beautiful parts of her body. Her hand that touches it. She, the conductor. If she's to repeat in the story — I'm thirsty — anybody, even the most ragged of them, will join lips to hers in order to leave her satisfied.

She would be enraptured and no camera would duplicate her expression.

2

He asked me: — What is the purpose of a city square?
I looked in surprise at this man who had asked me such a strange question and told him a little annoyed: — For kids to play in.
But his gaze remained riveted on mine and he said to me: — That's all?
— Well — I answered him — it's a green space, it brings oxygen into the area.
But just when I thought he was about to change the subject, he said to me: — You are sure that's all it's really for? Think a little harder. Then I really started to force myself to recall the few times I had spent any time there, what I'd seen, and I replied: — Actually, it's a place for recreation, even though lots of lovers come there too, now that I think about it, it's also full of lovers.
— And what do lovers do in the public square?
— They kiss and hug, I told him.
— And what else do they do there? he continued.
— Sometimes I've seen them touching their bodies, I answered.
— What do you mean by touching their bodies? insisted the other one.
— They caress each other, said the one they were interrogating.
— And precisely where does this take place? said the questioner.
— Usually they're sitting on benches in the square, although sometimes they're leaning against the trees but that doesn't happen as often. They touch by caressing each other while seated on the benches.
That's how they do it.
The interrogation seemed to come to an end, or at least, the silence pointed to that. That's why, when the other one raised his voice, the one being interrogated was startled.
— And what else have you seen in the square? he asked forcefully.
The one interrogated hesitated a few moments before answering: — I've seen elderly people sitting on the benches too, especially when it's sunny there are lots of elderly people, he said.
— And what do the elderly people sitting on the benches do? How long do they stay there? asked the interrogator.
— They don't do anything, they think, but if somebody sits down beside them they try to strike up a conversation,

maybe that's why they're always alone or else sitting in twos and threes, but never talking to each other, they only talk when their neighbor on the bench isn't elderly, replied the one being interrogated.

— But you didn't answer the whole question, said the other one. — How long do they stay there?

— For hours at a time, he answered.

— Who else comes to the square? persisted the one who was interrogating him.

He was running out of answers. He had to concentrate once again on his scant observation of the square until an image came to mind. That's how come he said confidently:

— Beggars, some beggars show up there. He said that.

— Beggars? And what do they do?

— They stretch out on the grass and I've seen some doing that on the benches. They'll sleep face to the sun when there is any, or else if it's winter and it's cold, they'll cover themselves with rags or newspapers, said the one they were interrogating.

— And the others, are they bothered by their presence?

— Nobody goes near them and if kids do, their mothers call them. Wherever they are a vacant space opens up. I think I heard once that it's against the law to sleep in city squares, said the interrogated one with a hint of enthusiasm in his voice.

— Who else, asked the interrogator, shows up there?

He thought he wouldn't come up with another answer. What else could there be in the square except for a few people killing time? Good God, who else goes to that place. Still he knew he had to answer, better for him at any rate, that's why he said:

— Some kooks, a few crazies come there who stay as long as the rest but unlike the others, they talk to themselves or even make incoherent speeches — he was expressing himself more freely now — but the people, even if they keep away from them, they don't have the same attitude as toward the beggars, as if they knew none of them's going to do them any harm. They don't show up that often, but it's not so unusual to see them there either.

— And how do you know they're crazy? asked the one doing the questioning. — Well, he answered, it's easy: by their actions, by what they say. I don't know, there's something in their eyes that makes it impossible to mistake them. You can see right away that they're sick, they're off their rocker, they're some place else, they've got their mind someplace else.

— Do you remember any one of them in particular? inquired the interrogator.

— No, no one in particular. They're like types to me, as if they came in a lump sum, he said, or maybe it's always the same one who shows up shabbier each time.

He did not know what else might come out if they went on like this. He was already astonished at having included the insane in the square since in reality, he had hardly ever noticed them. His stopping in the square had always been a break between one thing and another and as such, the place never commanded his attention. That's why it seemed to him now that it was a kind of unconscious observation that was surfacing and that he had seen a great deal more than he had realized. That's just how things were. But he was sure the questions had come to an end. But no. The voice rose again in order to say:

— All right, we'll go over it all again, this time in an orderly and coherent fashion. Describe the square, but just that: describe it objectively.

It was absurd, absolutely absurd, that's what it was. He was not going to go on with this game, that's why he said:

— No, I won't do it, it's idiotic.

The interrogator looked at him and told him:

— Do it. That is all he said.

— It's a square space, answered the one they were interrogating — its floor cemented over, more precisely, paved in gray squares with a design in the same color. There are tall, very old trees and grass. Around the edges are set benches, some stone, others wood. The wooden benches are painted green and harmonize with the color of the lawn and the branches of the trees. Some of these benches are damaged from use, missing beams in the backrest or slats from the seats themselves. The ones in good condition are the stone benches, bound to be because of what they're made of.

— And the cables for the electric lighting and the lampposts? said the interrogator: you haven't seen them by any chance?

— Yes, that's true, replied the other one, there are cables and lampposts. The cables are visible in the tree branches and the lampposts are set around the square. They're painted green too. But they don't lend themselves to closer scrutiny. Their function becomes clear at night when the light's turned on.

— And what effects do they have when the light is turned on? said the one interrogating him.

— The square looks phantasmagoric, like something unreal, he said.

To give an example it looks like some scene in an operetta or a space for putting on plays. It's all very desolate then.

— Have you been there at night? he asked, I mean: have you stayed there?

— No, he said, I've never stayed there at night, I've only passed by when I've been walking somewhere else, but stay there, never.

— All right, said the interrogator. We'll drop this point for the moment, but tell me then, in the daytime: who comes to the square?

He had to play along. In this situation the right thing to do was not let anger or weariness get the better of him. Obedience was what was called for.

That's why he calmly answered:

— I've seen kids playing there, accompanied by their mothers or nursemaids who keep an eye on them while sitting on the benches in the square. They talk among themselves, glancing from time to time at the children who mostly stay close by. Some of the very little ones fall down and give themselves a wallop on the concrete, then the mothers or the person in charge of them gets up and consoles them until the crying stops. Sometimes they fight with each other which obliges the grownup who's taking care of them to get up from their bench, interrupting the conversation in order to separate them. The children like the lawn a lot, they roll across it, pull it up and that way not only get their hands dirty but their clothes as well. Sometimes their mothers don't see them until the children come closer and then they say reproachful things to them. Some mothers knit and others even do embroidery and they carry food for the little kids in their bags. In the afternoon they get up, saying goodbye, and leave holding the children in their arms or by the hand. The exact time depends on the weather, but unless it's raining there are always children in the square.

He said it all at once, like a well-learned lesson, in a soft voice the way you would recite a piece of good literature, that's how he said it.

— But elderly people also come into the square, he went on, they're always bundled up, winter or summer. They're alone and looking to sit next to someone in order to strike up a conversation. The children are always the pretext, but generally the other person changes seats and that's why it's common to see two or three old people sharing the same bench in silence. They prefer the wooden benches, avoiding the stone ones. They stay there for several hours gazing from side to side. The women also knit and the men half read the newspaper, since their gaze is distracted by the general panorama of the square. Frequently they go off, leaving the paper carefully folded on the bench.

He thought he ought to add a lot more about them, he could do it, but he did not.

— Lovers also come there, he said. Couples who sit on the benches holding hands. They talk very slowly and from time to time they kiss. Sometimes they're sitting on the same bench as some older person who, visibly annoyed, looks the other way. The couples laugh and the woman caresses some kid when playing brings him near.

Now and again the square is also the setting for the end of some affair. They talk for a long time and sometimes the woman cries without hiding it. Then the man sits there visibly embarrassed because of the others who are gazing at the scene and he hugs the woman, not as a loving gesture but to shield her from the gaze of strangers, as if he feared the others might blame him. At these moments the woman forgets the surroundings, but the man is hanging on what the others might think of him. Generally the man convinces the woman to leave quickly and she leaves the square crying.

Other couples who meet in secret can also be observed. They sit on the benches farthest away, check the time often, and uneasiness conditions each one of their actions. These couples always seem to be at the point of breaking up. One of the two is there under compulsion, seeming to need a more intimate spot, but paradoxically there are lots of them in the square, like a prologue to something. They don't stay long, but they always follow a different rhythm from the rest of the square. They do not regard the rest of the people, presumably for fear of their furtiveness being discovered. They lower their faces when a gaze crosses theirs. In short, they're there in spite of themselves as a way to dilute playing with chance.

But some young people embrace without concealing it. They let themselves get swept over the threshold of their sexuality. These couples also remove themselves to the most distant benches, or they stretch out on the grass and their bodies rub against each other. They avoid the others' gaze and their hands slide subtly. But their faces betray them. You might realize that possession is imminent, that desire spreads in the square.

He interrupted himself. With lowered eyes he said: — I'm thirsty.
The one who was interrogating him replied:
— Later, finish first.
— But not just young people spread their desire in the square, various ages are always present according to the different intensities with which they expose their shameless-ness.
He thought that once again he still might add a lot more, but he decided to keep some things in reserve. Besides there was still a lot to say about the people in the square and his thirst was growing.
Just the reverse, he ought to synthesize more, to save the maximum number of words, being sure about what he wanted to express.
— Beggars, he said, come into the square and stay there for stretches at a time. Sometimes they even come in groups. People are afraid of them and keep their children from going near them. They're threatening presences, not just because of the danger of aggression but also because of the chance of catching some disease they might spread by rubbing up against them or coming close. They don't beg. They even sleep there covered with rags or just newspapers that protect their bodies on freezing days. The bench doesn't matter to them, it can be wood or stone. They sleep with their mouths open and very deeply. Others come back to the place at different times of day, as if they had something to do and were returning to the square to rest. It's possible that they go to some bar nearby. That's very possible, since almost all of them are drunks. They look wasted and stricken with age. The women keep their children away and those people don't even try to strike up a conversation with anyone. They recognize that they're set apart from the rest. But, nevertheless, they're rightfully there by virtue of its being a public place. Also it's well

known, their disregard for the others and their enormous capacity for lack of connection with the surroundings. Frequently they also start rearranging things in the bag they carry and even take out some torn-up rags and bandage their legs which I've seen ulcerated and injured. If they're in the middle of that and some kid comes up to them, the mother or whoever's minding them quickly snatches the kid away, scolding them and explaining in a loud voice that never, but never should they go near those people, who are dangerous, who are sick. Their ages are indeterminate, and well, they're always coming and going.

To the others who also ring the square he ought to add the students, the people on foot, but it would be endless. Unless it became absolutely necessary he would not do it. The other's gaze incited him to continue, impatience was beginning to show in his eyes, that's why he said:

— Some crazies also show up and people maintain a different attitude toward them than to the beggars. Not because these come near them, no, because pity mixed with irony and amazement are evident in them. As for them, they're characterized by their incoherent speeches that can be heard in various intonations. Some, even virulent. They're dressed like the beggars, but with more exaggerated touches. They don't look at the others either. Even though their harangues are crossed by insults of a public that never corresponds to the one listening to them. Life in the square isn't changed by their arrival. After a while they go away and the sound of their voices lingers after their figures.

— That's what I know about the square, I couldn't add anything else.

The interrogator got up from his seat and looked down at him, obliging him to raise his head and said to him:

— You're tired, friend.

— Yes, said the one being interrogated.

— You'll rest for now, later, you still have some questions to answer. And raising the pitch of his voice he asked him:

— Who comes into the public square?

— Children, the people accompanying them, lovers, the elderly, a few beggars, occasionally some kook, answered the one they were interrogating.

— Describe the square, said the interrogator.

— Trees and benches, concrete squares, lawn, electric cables, street lamps, replied the other.

— How late do people stay there?
— Until nightfall, the last of the natural light, until the street lights are turned on.
— When is the square empty?
— On rainy days, at night, in those circumstances nobody stays in the square, he responded.
— Come on, tell the truth: are the beggars so different from the crazies?
— Actually they're not totally different from each other, but the crazies are always talking, they seem worked up, but there's something they have in common that passes across their features, in the self-abandon they display, the one being interrogated answered wearily.

The interrogator kept silent a few moments and his voice rose again:
— At what time does the electric light come on?
— I don't know exactly, but its being turned on is the same across the whole city. When the square lights up all the streets in Santiago are also being lit up.

Something had definitely snapped. The questions were getting more and more trivial. But it was not something to get into a discussion about. So far as he could he was going to answer about whatever matter he was questioned on. Because something depended on that, or why else would the other man take that tone: the boldness of his gaze, the lack of facial expressions, the professionalization of this situation. Maybe it was to humiliate him or the prelude to getting at something significant and then he would be so tired that he would say, beg and ask for water, because his thirst would be unbearable by then. That's why he shifted his eyes swiftly when the one interrogating him said:
— I too have been there and that's exactly why you'll understand how all this could open up and lead one way or another to the inevitable conclusion. So that's why we're not building this thing up. Tell me:
— What have you seen when the light is turned on?
— I've seen nothing.
— Nothing? I saw the takes and what's more, took them apart down to the point of disjointing them, frame by frame. It was an excessively long time while the beam of light struck my head, but even so I was there until I finished that job.

So that was it, thought the one being interrogated, that's

where his attitude came from. It all got simpler if the guy had seen the takes. Which permitted him to say:

— Yes, I saw you and recognized you from the very first moment. When the camera shot you maybe your pose was different, but no doubt about it, it was a very typical gesture of yours upstaging that whole angle:

when she was on the verge of falling and the arm of the man who stopped her was stretched out. That's how they were until he, who was bending over her, said some words to her, with her face wet with tears and it was a confession that E. Luminata hurled into the middle of the square at that man who was listening to her, enveloped in her gray dress, with her razed head down and her mouth almost in the ear of the man who was indeed prepared for this incident.

Then they laid out the cables to set up the scene. Fused into one landscape and character, writing and medium, an error as well to praise it.

What would he say:

Nothing he might say would make the one held up stumble and, still, the simple familiar gesture of bringing her mouth close to the ear of a stranger could excite passion in others — in her despair — Imagine saying something that way to a perfect stranger.

To lay her preference bare to another.

It was an ongoing mistake because her voice was low and the cars that kept passing by drowned out her words. He half listened and completed with his thoughts and desires what he wanted to hear.

He changed words, suppressed whole phrases, cut important speeches, thinking them secondary. He could not extend himself to totalities. Not even heed her gestures, eager as he was to be consumed in their contents.

But let's forget about the superfluous, the fourth scene is being set up:

Let's put it this way.

The projection of two simultaneous scenes.

1. Interrogator and interrogated.
2. The fall of E. Luminata.

But perhaps one might be fused with the other and that way it's the man (any man) who was at the point of falling in the square and another man (any other man) quickly got up from his seat and grabbed hold of him to prevent his striking against the cement and after that, maybe, the victim of the accident confessed the reason for his distraction: that it was due to a few drinks too many and the other might think how he had helped a mere drunk.

But if that's not how it was either and that first man had been sick, really sick, looking for some place to rest and, nevertheless, did not manage to make it even to the bench in the square and now, thanks to the rescuing hand, reached it and rested a while until every trace of the illness disappeared.

Although it might have been weariness that made him stumble and, on account of the embarrassing situation he was not even grateful for the assistance and without looking at the other sat down to recover his energies.

If that happened, then the fall in the square would be subverted and it would be she perhaps whom they interrogated and not a single word would have come from her mouth, because interrogation here is a sacred word and only in the camera would her expression have been appraised.

If she instead did the interrogating, it would have been a confusing business. For all these reasons, replacing this scene would be out of the question.

Even if it were inserted like a backdrop, scene over scene: interrogator and interrogated. It will make use of these secret words. They are already catalogued on magnetic tape so as to be scanned as possible dialogue, as surreptitious elements.

It's true, somebody at that time was being interrogated. Perhaps they touched lightly on that business in the square. He even could have told all he saw there: their demonstrations, the marches, the zeal of those people. He will identify some faces from pictures. They will have changed. They will be aged by the paleness that characterizes them and even he will be recognized in those photographs or in the shots of those fans.

It might be like that, or rather that's how it is. Because in these cases each document is an indication or a proof, but it is impossible not to leave signs. The love of photography is known. Someone will no longer be there, a few names will be rubbed out in the Kardex and the Kardex destroyed and the square will cease being important. It will go back to being decoration for the city.

Even if it's filmed.
The face is imprinted on celluloid by another technique. The photographers keep arriving and they film the kids, their mothers and even some beggar as background. But at night, at night it's something else and it has already been said that the cold does not let them stay sitting on the benches or leaning against the trees and that's why, moving around, they raise their eyes toward the illuminated sign and dreaming believe that it warms them.

3

I

She moans at pitches that widen the crack in her aura, that tint
rather at punches by battle-hardened branches of her recep-
tacles. She groans, but that's not why she doesn't dislocate
herself, simply lets the wind pass through the grass that
identifies her greatest vocalizings, or maybe branches were
what produced a deceptive effect: the listener heard moans and
maliciously thought she was suffering/ but once aloft she let
herself be carried away, no that's not how it was. She was
posing with her voice extended into the plaza in order to erode
it with auditory strokes. She increases her effort, thrusts
forward her neck, gathers momentum — more intense
seductive power — for the one watching her who gets hooked
another way, yet leaving her to drag herself while making
noises, she falls and does not get up or snakes across maybe
again: drags herself and at the same time leaves her spittle
spread over the square's pathways/ she marks a route.

II

She cracks her ill-omened aura and still keeps intact the
savage incidence of her throat. She so upsets the one who
hears her in such noisy trotting or trampling that he becomes
conditioned. The branch delays these vibrations, the grass
feeds the pale green. Does the cable carry its energy? She
moos really just the way a cow does, moos and drags herself
along as in a birth sequence, but seizes her throat and draws
out still more of its sound. Something has happened for her
pitch to drop, the cow withdraws to her marginations, the mare
calms down, the thing that's come into being stops completely,
so that the grove, so pitiful in its sparseness, leaps into the
foregrounds/ the tree that nourishes her/ her muzzle scrapes to
reach the branches, she stains and annuls her muzzled shape,
marks time with the tip of her hoofs, raises high her haunch/
suckles herself.

III

She has her haunches punched/ scratched rather by her own
fingernails, pink trails establish fiery marks like proprietaries.
Rearing herself up she radiates sterile kicks. But she hurts her

feet against tree trunks when she tears up grass: she trembles, produces her mooings again, sinks down, stretches out, smoothes her thick coat. The mark is stamped into her shivers, the hide is singed — she trots again — injures herself against the stone bench by not gauging her trot, the electric light petrifies her and halts her under the lampposts; she rubs herself and her neighs grow louder when she smashes into that metal which, nonetheless, goes on with the absurd farce of producing her public illumination/ that's why she offers her haunch/ her muzzle/ her spittle which slides over the green bench. She moos and neighs copies those sounds/ covers those burns with her hands.

IV

The hearing gets jammed by the mixing — which sounds? which animal? which human can contrive her warbling? — disorients rather the listener; it rigs and swaps its indelible compass in descending to the vile condition that possesses her. Spurred on as she is in the experiment when she trots or gallops in order to satisfy herself. She yields none of her arrogance when crossing over to another species and another animal state. By means of sound, her body changes its behavior/ the square then grows dangerous: that corral which transforms it into a pen, lamppoles into posts, benches into rails to the point of flaying the legs that look wrapped as though for a gala race. She marks her haunch with scratches, her hair lets pink zones show through as the grass does with the ground. But, which look is coming next? She breaks into a gallop/ barbed wire holds her back.

V

A filly in heat needs a stud, but this one's no good for such stages, it's pasture perhaps for bestializing. She brings her mouth closer, copying her orifice, stretches her neck delicately, a double gesture renewed in its constancy/ muzzle and voice run by simultaneously: the one listening to her insists on the moaning, the one looking at her suffers from all the flaying, the one reading her linear seeks ritual, the one thinking her desires the haunches. Her mane lengthens, the hairs on her legs stand up, stiffen, rasp, and sink in. She

stretches the hairs like decorative festoons so as to test that
way their resistance, she bends her legs, showing the notches
in her hoofs that damage the green grass, her sound is different
on concrete. Her hide is hidden by hair, it mocks the cold and
so this stay in the square becomes bearable. In her animal state
she wins the stay.

VI

In her animal course she is gaited slow as though she really
were on offer, twitches off flies for lined-up lumpen, her
haunches tremble to transport them; she becomes stained,
broadens, fattens, grows stronger to really support this
mounted pack, approaching neighs at them, moos at them,
scraping the concrete with those hoofs/ trots/ gallops to fire
them up, tempting them with such business. But this new
image palls and before that she gently draws close to them:
bends her legs lowers her head against the pavement, moos in
a soft tone or surely it's meowing, close to her purring resorts
to the lawn as her background and sweats from her new
image/ from the cold yearns for lumperratic fusion, but out of
greed keeps on grazing; watches those other forms at a
distance, licks the lack of that weight on her haunches/ her
look is incomplete without them mounted on her.

VII

She scours the rubbish for her saddle, starts to run the square
again. Nothing's any good to her that might serve to confine
her expanded contexture or shield it from the violent jabs.
What decoration on the haunches might prove irresistible? In
what circumstance would spurs dig into her flanks? Mounting
her/ riding her/ exhausting her or maybe hurrying her gently
on with the metal points to her hip. Not in vain does she
quicken her stride when examining all the holes in the
public square. More insistent when under the lamp, less when
near the benches/ she almost rubs against those stiffened
boards, but averts her gaze so as to surprise them/ makes this
run listlessly. But her eyes stay fixed on the ground and
although she does not cease exhibiting her haunches, as if that
were involuntary, she knows she still can be mounted bareback.

VIII

Sweat against sweat would sink in, a salty taste the rubbing of flesh till there's a wound if her haunches supported that lumpenpack without saddle. She'd turn in circles so the spurs would punish her, that way the others' rumps would be packed onto her own haunches, to give them a view of the square from a privileged height. If it were mounted on her she would bear it with opened legs but clamped tight against her side, stop it under the lamp to bring a glow to its face. But that would be secondary in the final analysis: she would stop following orders, would twist her path by threatening to crash into the trees or rather against benches instead, always disobey the command of other legs, so that her feet would mark a path different from the mounted's. Until at last she would feel in her sides the rage of the spurs, the relentless penetration of the metal and then only would she be able to neigh, moo, bellow, feel the wound.

IX

But to neigh, moo, bellow before the spurs stab into her flanks, only a moment before responding to the imperceptible, to cause the event's truth to be constructed only in reverse action or why not, studio editing, movie maybe or pure sound. The professional's hands on the keyboard, his enthusiasm over his discovery — she mooed and she bellowed deafened with her neighs — She roughly throws off the saddle, reins in her trot, stiffens her haunch, doubles back to the edges of the square. She lies down again and licks that thick coat to add luster to her look. She then gambols across the lawn, raises her hoofs as though frolicking, opens the muzzle-shaped mouth pointed toward the lamp for the fortified gleam of her teeth. She stays there as though killing time but in reality offering her product/ the animal incites its mounting.

X

We have her once again on the grass diminished in image, stopped in flight. Her project's taken a tumble: because of her need for a watering trough; sweating through her hair has dehydrated her. All the trotting, straining with the throat, all

the showing herself off has, in short, left her exhausted.
Programming the mounting has plunged her beforehand into
extreme weariness. Where to drink in this space? Concrete on
the ground, grass, so, where to hatch her watering place? What
container could hold her water? Having reached this particular
stage and not being able to overcome this crude obstacle, she
is about to fail in her undertaking. She rejected her success —
almost ruins her business — to turn back to the razed head, her
thin down, her meek behavior, the delicate voice that characterized her, her hegemony over lumpen. But she pulls herself
together on realizing that even the best animals get winded.

XI

That's why she lets a few moments pass until the sweat
subsides, resting her throat lets the saliva moisten it, starting
to feel the cold in the square again, dragging herself then
across the concrete and starting to roll around on the
pavement's squares. Avoiding light directly on her head, that
light which at times produces heat delirium in a cold period.
She stretches out at full length on the frozen ground, lets her
hairs separate breaking the mix her sweat has constructed on
their surface. But she doesn't hurry in bringing that about, she
wants to start with her sounds once her throat is wound up.
She feels the saliva penetrating it, it is slowly moistened/ now
she swallows/ the liquid turns it slippery, she finds herself in
shape for emitting noises so essential to her scaling. That's
why she opens her muzzle briefly and practices her neigh.

XII

She breaks into a new trot more cautious still, more pleasing
the peculiar sound from those concrete squares that better
situate her hoofs. She circles trees to work herself up, her neck
rises toward the branches, her muzzle avidly seeks the green,
her haunches tremble meanwhile to enable her solid mass to
get by. She trots them in fine style, without going near certain
benches set among lamppoles while the pale people gather at
the far end. She takes care to remain in the absolute center of
that square — the electric light is truer there — perhaps the
only locatable point. All of a sudden she halts her trot and
right in the center pokes with her hoof. It's her signal call

more than a search. Her neck lowers, her haunches rise, her hairs undergo a gentle bristling. Predictably her broad hoofs begin their unchecked gallop in the very center of the plaza.

XIII

She's the mare let loose and her hair glistens dangerously; besides doing harm to herself, she could harm the square if she doesn't organize her tracks right. The hoofs resound deafeningly. Her body stretches as she stretches her legs: she crosses, punches holes, shows herself swift, expert as well in surmounting obstacles. Her first jump over the stone bench which she discharges superbly; her large body, faultless, takes on this transfer to the other point where the lumperrant stratum keeps itself. She snorts and she sweats although her thick coat looks shiny still: it's thin water that her exuberance as active animal does not succeed in shaking off. Far reaching is her gallop that moves so solid an obstacle only in the equine way, when constraint has compelled her to arrive quickly before her riders, making it appear that she is tearing herself away from them and that it's her wrong course that pushes her right to the center of the silvery spur.

XIV

She makes the rounds of their bodies when showing herself at a moderate gait before their figures, she parades now as before the race at which bettors would have waited to measure her, weigh her and wager on her. She wants, no doubt, to make a sweep of their pick and for them she acts a bit skittish, shows her skill, her craft in the parade to the gate, raises her haunch, turns her chest, tosses her neck, announces the triumph resulting from her good breeding and even snorts, scratching the ground with the dexterity of her hoof that tears up grass, pulls out soil. They do not follow her lead any farther: actually the lumpen have fallen back before her broadside, they deny her effect, show themselves deaf to her sounds, rub their hands to fight off the cold, retreat in an obvious way to the place where her presence cannot be observed by them, seeing her as filly still, not cow or mare.

XV

But she does not go back on her needs, she knows it's hard to
get started making a break from their obsolete rites — but she
does not back away — nor is she confused because they
ignore her, she knows that thanks to the power of her haunch,
she will manage to hold those other legs bareback and their
own bodies will be lost. It's her performance that's at stake:
that expert animal aptitude that's moved into the public
square, all that space belonging to her where she has practiced
her best poses. She waits for the stroke to descend, rubs her
neck against the trees, or shrinks back into the dark space. She
stays still for leading astray, knows that now they are looking
for her. She moos in the miserable-looking grass, more pitiful
than everything attained so far; he who hears her outside the
plaza blames the wind, whereas lumpen fall prey to the
delusion that maybe she suffers when she moos and that truly
she has been able to reach the cow barn.

XVI

She moos in a hospitable tone seeking that way the other
vicinity, a complicitous sound matches hers and she moos with
her raised neck, with her lamentable muzzle in which blades
of grass fill in holes. She raises her pitch, broadcasts her howl,
calls and advertises herself in her despair — copies a sick
animal — tinctures a beast in heat, although her throat really is
capable of attaining the neigh. Now they are ready for her
appearance, her ribs are polished to a shine, she longs then for
the mounting so as to link it with the marking by fire; her own
mark its own master, its design private signs. That's why she
must perform her ritual when it has come to pass, the fleshing
state, she being called upon to leave her haunch crossed by
those animal scratches.

XVII

But, who'll mount her? who'll drive spurs into her? who'll
hurt her? what lumpen'll seize that right? what legs? what
haunches place themselves over hers? That choice troubles her
at the brusque interruption of the constant, if there are no other
faces than that of the electric light which rules the wakeful

square. And what if it was the light that moaned her? if light
alone mounted her? With one stroke at full potency he would
flay her flank and even if the gleam of the silvered spur was
lost, the penetrating metal leapt out of her with the bucking
from that electric banging, single/ infallible that reproached
her for even thinking about the effectiveness of her demolition, which stretched her out on the pavement in spasmodic
displays from the impact. If the mysterious cable punched her
stuffed side with no other sign than the sudden fall that left no
mark but the burn on her side.

XVIII

She leaves them then with the drool dangling, when they were
so close to the contact of climbing on top of her, of augment-
ing the wallop with the gallop that had been announced. That's
not how it'll be: her perfect haunch isn't about to support their
meager flesh, nor has her brute style been established merely
to acquiesce in dark trotting so that some lumpen or other can
go overboard till she's left exhausted along the benches.
Because those others, who would hold them back? She should
spend the night galloping, and maybe, half blind from the
walloping, wreck herself against those benches or tossing and
pitching among the lampposts, tearing up the grass even more.
And her flanks would be a ruin even greater than the square is
now, and what's worse, the strength of the neigh would be
diluted in order to be superimposed over the motors of cars
already passing by at dawn. That's not how it'll be: nobody
will compel her to choose lumpen.

XIX

But how to entice electric light? with what mechanism disturb
it? If she neighs, if she moos or roars, if she stretches herself
out lazily like a tabby, if she drags along like an insect at the
limits of the lamplight, if she croaks, if she chirps, will it get
results? make that cable cobble her bareback? interrupt the
light for one moment? Because if the light condensed on her
body, then she could take any form, the vilest; it could leave
her haunches or the strength of the moo diminished in pres-
ence/ it could come to burying in her mind the purity of the
gallop. If the cable touched her then, darkness would be the

incipient manner of the square and she would come back to life that way as a blue specter, alone in the center like a living advertisement, like a product in illuminated flesh. Now she would manage the burns in return for the privilege of her brief ad: she would sell herself fully, entirely open, every sound would come out of her gullet.

XX

And what would become of that illuminated sign? His pure architecture would fall into shadows, cables then like dead matter, having extracted the colors from it. The switching between the sign's sections will not cast any more letters, the sign will be nothing but an absurd wooden scaffold, a useless formula atop the building. She would be the only salable material, sole desire among lumpen, the same letter on her body in the meaning most enigmatic, most inaccessible, another product would be established amid the sound from her erected trumpeter. Because neither her moos nor the expert power of neighing have managed to dilute the strong mark of that luminous sign which had robbed her of her only presence before pale people shielded behind its letters. She would turn it off yes, if to herself she could attract that energy, just like that the cut, with such spirit, that she would receive his full potency: it would pass over her singed side.

XXI

She's the one now who loses hope, looks for the cut, splits herself variously, moos one more time at the light, like a she-wolf prolongs her howls, uncoils like a reptile before the lamp, shifts from haunch to haunch in successive moments, expands and contracts, takes on her natural gray color when she withdraws from a mulish look, links up phonetic noises from her throat until they approach human sounds. She changes, prances dampness from her eyes, keeps her hoofs for furiously perforating the green lawn. She kicks, slithers, damages the benches still further, splintering some of their wood. She grows frenzied with her own strength, snorts and sweats, shuns the cold. She has forgotten about the pale people in performing her temptation of the electric light. But no, that's not entirely so. This omission is necessary in order to fully

achieve the autonomy of shining without hinderance, with no
light other than that of her own hides.

XXII

But she couldn't give up the haunch, not suddenly like that
with the trot or the sublime presence of the mooing. Her lying
down bovine has unstrung her when putting on speed she has
sensed the long reach of her hoofs grazing grass. The holes in
the ground, the fragile bench that has been splintered in the
butting. Losing that power in the throat frightens her, taking
full possession of her ribs, mere lateral bones that do not attain
the mein of galloping. Any state, bovine or equine and even
mulish is more prized. Maintaining herself in it indefinitely
would lend elegance to her mooing, class she'd achieve in
neighing, a meek appearance if she were to bray. It's all there,
the jump she made over the bench before, free, clean, perfect.
She has crossed the square's barrier, passed from one corral to
another.

XXIII

She exists in clear distinction from the luminous advertisement that more than ever appears in the static state of two
parallel ads. That is, she has sought for herself an animal
multiformity when she came to superimposing roaring upon
mooing and the neighs. In a single voice that emanated from
her own throat, without waiting for the energy that would
allow her a second stage. If she achieved it through her own
vocal power, every other option would seem a step back in her
harmony. And the spur? It would have left nothing in her
horsiness to chance, giving a meaning to the roughness of her
neigh. The grass has already favored her bovine being when
she stretched out her bulky forms on the lawn, the gray of the
pavement has mimeticized her in her mulish business, her
humble trot. But mare above all else she doesn't fulfill herself
if her haunch remains untamed. Bucking, shaking, throwing
that rider off her haunch

XXIV

It resolves into a dichotomous problem. Either the electric

cable or the obstinate spur. If she opted for the spur the electric light would be what illuminates the entrance of the steel into her ribs. A pure fragment would be established, the cut to a piece of her flank, the spur that draws close, grazes her, pulls back until roughly it penetrates her, piercing her abundant coat. Again the spur and the split flesh that cracks and will be tamed into an animal wound. Two mountings: the rider himself and the other who aims at her with the camera, but not at the whole beast, just at the flank. Or perhaps she would resist like a young mare and throw them down off her flank with the intensity of her gallops and the threatening spur could not penetrate her. They walk by and check, they line up to mount her, the lumpen itself is roaring/ is about to jump the fence.

XXV

Her corral she knows well and also the barriers that hold her back. Even without electric light she would be able to lead a bull's-eye gallop along its borders. But the lumpen is also master of these concrete squares; they would be able to retrace their steps even if the electric light failed. She backs into one of the corners to decide which path is hers. The square grows darker, the lamps give another luminosity to the lawn, the trees are what mark the height, the benches appear as signs. She withdraws to a corner and weaves her plot, she controls herself, the horseshoes on her hoofs improve the sound of her race. That's just why she runs again, just why she shows off on the pavement deliberately, without getting worked up her trumpet-snouted mouth does not snort, her coat's flawless, there's not a trace. She looks toward the edges of the square, sees lumpen. She is surrounded by the silveriness of their multiple spurs: they surround her.

XXVI

But she decides nothing yet: now neither bellows at them nor moos at them, now does not tempt them. Total confusion could lead her to a pitiful end, to an ugly scene. She devotes herself solely to the pleasure of her sound on the concrete surface, to its broad structure in which for the first time the edges are precise limits. She moves her belly, stretches and opens her chest, ignores lumpen who have managed to see her, denies herself even to the illuminated sign also casting his words at her. She gazes attentively at the lamps whose scant light scumbles her. She's in a comfortable position. Dodging she finds commitment, once again she's delighted with these shapes; she tries to postpone her decision. Simply being there in the square like just any walker of the streets merely taking a stroll or lying down or mooing if something gives her pleasure. Trotting as well if the cold lays siege, blotting out the camera's expectation, avoiding a brush with the scene.

XXVII

The one listening to her thinks the weather's gotten worse, but those lumpens show their ironies by slamming spurs heel against heel. They want to rival her sounds with the peculiar note struck by steel in this corral. A melody could almost be made out: her trotting on the concrete squares and along the edges the song of the steel; they clap her, dance her, celebrate her those lumpens, they keep her going round in circles with their spurring, she eases the trot, softens it to the point of responding to their sounds in that rhythm which is curveting. She also slackens so as to annoy them, holds the trot down to the long step, but that melody obliges her to accelerate her hoofs in keeping time. She is celebrating in an inevitable way, burning too in her central presence — tints herself rose in the image of a dancer — watches her step/ monitors the fall.

XXVIII

The celebration stops. She deduces her precarious image, the scene is directed by her aura which is reconstructed again in laric spaces, in trills or moos her horse height curves conquered croup. But if with brusque leaps she trepans her corral the slats of the benches creak and in a stupor she stumbles. Her keenest desire is not the spur, it is illusory or a light screen that is spread out, her volume diminishes in the eddies, the spur and the rider, yes they put up with it but not this animal that breaks loose. She rumbas it's true, though not in a foreign rhythm since her vacacination mark gives her its own action, she neither dances nor raises her rump: other means she uses, those stakes keep her from her flank, she matures it herself, the hairy coat is blind just like her search for the water-trough. The animal acts from instinct, erects itself and butts without bristling her neck, breaks her horns — maybe — on smashing lamppoles/ neither the light, nor the product of that illuminated sign disturbs her numbed mind/ the animal fears only red.

XXIX

There's no duality for the beast, her ardor is there on the lawn which she rakes, jail cell and jute cord lowered which her haunch cracks when punched with her feverish mark, the fire, the iron that burns is going to transfer its hegemony. So the beast does not sell herself to easy cattle rustling, the beast goes back to the homestead and grazes. Her hoof on the ground is provisional, the nape of her neck overcome by sleep. The animal at pasture directs the scene, the concrete is dangerous domain, it injures, it cracks that horseshoe from the nail, penetrates harmlessly through the holes. They hammer at her with the growth, from filly to mare, shoed she wanders once more. The trees stand higher than her neck stretching for the branches: her haunch, her hindquarters have no purpose beyond the obstinate mark on her posterior sign; she dirties and stains, tints with her remains of brutishness from her sick piebald. They hang jingling bells on the old nag.

XXX

Dappled the mare shows herself and her square space is the brightly lit corral/ her own hoofs scrape against her to keep her from ending up a strange crossbreed/ she spreads open her belly, suckles herself, without shame or fear sucks her haunch. The mosquitoes drive her crazy or maybe those horseflies were her trots that gesticulated her, her piebald state, her scrawny stain, her muzzle is animal humored, the grass fattens her all's set what weight? what fat? The animal grows more deformed yet: they mark her again and it's her intention to free her feet/ they shear her in their processes, the beast roars. Also the one in heat — she doesn't suffer — moos all she can and although neon bars push her out, with her present instinct she gets hot under the pressure of her hair, nurses herself still and turns more piebald yet. Thorse-flavored slice of her flesh is not offered as merchandise/ the furrow plows the ground.

XXXI

The illuminated sign does not offer meats, Kardexes or tapes that twirl/ the animal pays no mind, trots all it can, sniffs the dangerous form, slides the bundle away. She has no name other than that of her class. The piebald mare rises to her feet, the filly that has been's tended to, they pace her, puff her up on fat in the corral, her spur-stabbed ribs hollow from hunger. The lumperratic animal does not butt or charge, this animal of near-blind stock yields to the fire's mark, to the posts/ the barriers renew her, she tries out her horn, the benches are worn away, this animal stuck to the ground scratches herself on the grass and the haunch's power is worn down. The branches/ they snore the snort if she's been taught it. But it is the regulated force, even the rearing can be anticipated. The animal deaf to the sound, distant, frigid behavior. The animal couples with another naturally pours herself out/ the mare's reduced to her ankles, if the mare falls down/ if the animal breaks it's good for nothing.

4

Toward the Formation
of an Image in Literature

4.1   TOWARD THE FORMULATION OF AN IMAGE IN LITERATURE

So then/

We Chileans, we look for messages
E. Luminata, undividedly she
Thinks about Lezama and rubs them together
With James Joyce rubs them together
With Neruda Pablo rubs them together
With Juan Rulfo rubs them together
With E. Pound rubs them together
With Robbe Grillet rubs them together

With any Tom, Dick or Harry rubs antennae.

in that the one in the square, she turns her head in successive
movements — seated on the bench — with feet crossed on the
ground. Interrupted for the eye focused on her by pedestrians
and farther away by cars that obstruct her. Her head freezes to
the left or right, but without losing its monotonous regularity.

4.2   TOWARD THE FORMULATION OF AN IMAGE

To spend the rest of her days in a hospital room sedated and
fed artificially by means of serum, with her body covered and
her face scumbled under a sheet of plastic, which inside the
tent would absorb it.

To spend the rest of her days like a vegetable until the inef-
fable moment of her death. Expelling all her sufferings so as to
pass them on to the beings who precede her. Without staining
them with the scar. By sheer will power to impregnate the
injury: madness from her loss when she reappears as a
terminal patient, never again to glimpse Santiago de Chile,
forgetting the future like a tombstone.

With knees pressed together at the spasm, in order to turn
herself into purity. To bury her obscene thoughts.

To confirm that her soul can disappear in this state, since it
was an invention that was offered in propitiation to each dawn/
which she took such care of; her soul wrought like a gem that
is enlarged in a hospital room and evaporated outside the tent,
erratic toward lumpen, would stick to other bodies, bogging
them in its poison.

They needing her, she lacking care, astonished at her new
condition, withdrawn from her twin invention at its transposi-
tion, she calls herself E. Luminata and grows more astonished.

Stretched out on the bed with her prolix hair and her teeth, or
those eyes that have learned too much about this territory.

Apparently overcome by sleep, although the flush spreads
over her cheeks, and those pale people don't touch her.

She to whom nothing has happened outside this quadrangle.

She remains bent over: her head clearly visible in the cervix of
the shot. They have observed her from her best angles,
instilling in her letter by letter, word by word, scripts and
performances, until with a blistered, broken tongue she was
able to recite the clearest speeches by reducing them to

memories, her mind like an archive. To lie that way in a
hospital room — stripped of all soul — far from the trees, with
the plastic that every so often falls over her face without her
own hand being able to remove it. But in the rubbing to repeat
the rebellious branches, which more than once were able to
hide her when all alone she got ready in the square to launch
one of her attacks.

That's how she could be — occupying that bed — while gazes
examine her vital signs and the instruments check her heartbeats. In that condition voluntarily, she poses.

Through her veins supplied, extracted in liquids through
catheters, and those hands that clean her from time to time,
smooth her hair, straighten the blankets.

Until the others get thoroughly soaked in her new condition
and it is no longer anything but a memory trace and naturalness takes over in her room: aseptic she lies disconnected from
all perfection, while the pale people come back into the square
and stretched out on the benches double her state with their
eyes closed, cutting her off from the passage of the electric
light. Scattered on the wooden and stone benches without
being possessed by sleep. And in each one of their mental
images, let it be she with her face covered, motionless and
innocent, who irradiates a uniform thought.

Let them be like that night after night each one uncomfortably
occupying one of the beds in the square, with rhythmic
breathing and arms extended for the serum, lacking souls:
posing, all of them.

While she, numbed between the sheets, any day now may
withdraw to the other world, which undoubtedly will reveal to
her the erroneousness of it all. Let white sheets snake across
the hospitable letters and let the hands of those miserable pale
people cut off the serum, undo the bandages and leave the cell
in darkness.

(from one of her images)

For example:

For that dawning to approach it takes as many hours as her
strangest thoughts: her physical condition deteriorating,
tortured, deluded by the imminent transformation which stuck
to her body trepans her skull.

When the next dawning of her corrupted corporal space is
presumed and even so there persists the same body com-
pressed in that razed head, with the maximum mawkishness
this still confined specter permits her. Her atoms that construct
her in a head razed smooth ready.

— Who knows what paths this runagate head is taking, —
because it's certain that she put it on so as not to exit half
dead, but scarcely transformed, scarcely dye cut, half warmed
up.

For that new dawning of an image in literature in which she
expresses herself head hanging down from her luminous
body. A head of perfect dimensions razed from front to back.

Stating what was thought inadmissible: that beneath her razed
skull lay hidden her true beauty
              her promiscuity
all her talent/ now one gets lost with all the switches that
prevent distinguishing what's faked from what's real.

She throws off the covers and thinks they are drilling her. She
stretches down square for them to puncture her bones and
that's even why they have left the razed head silent/ she pops
tranquilizers when the stabbing pains bother her, no longer
remembers very clearly and is left with the craziest dreams:
that she's flying.

Her head demolished by razing stabs.

With such powerful lights no one can escape her image. The
phosphorescent razed head is uncovered and an incoherent
conversation appears in memory's place/ pure shadows/ x-rays
against the light and they're hung up.

In that room any sound is eliminated other than that of her
head being drilled, because from opening the skull — all

blocked — her secrets are growing dimmer and dimmer. Now some of her memories are being nullified.

But she remains bound to the bed and at each spasmodic movement the straps around her are tightened.

Her legs rise in convulsive movements/ they settle her down/ her dreams surface through lip movements. Blood from her head tints the rags.

They change to snow-white rags and it booms.

But they are going to put her thoughts in order, because the strokes of electricity only left her — before — urinating and blinking beneath the glare from the light shaft when they assigned her a bed/ assigned her a chart.

— She was transferred to the terminal ward when nothing more could be done with her.

Upstairs she kept on uttering the same gibberish which no longer had any impact on the observers.

She fell entirely out of the square and into the middle of the light shaft and hoped they would call her, poke her, hoped anything at all really.

She lay with her hands fallen limp at her sides. She was the image of relaxation.

She remained unrecognizable in her terror of electricity expressed by elemental gestures — how to say it — scarcely blinked in the room when they were getting ready to make her comfortable. She forgot everything. Even the woman who closed her legs and back to the light shaft again, where a sunbeam fell on the big table and the fools insisted on contemplation at a scale of centimeters.

That was before.

She remains stretched out from the surgery/ the x-rays are against the light showing the defect.

Maybe that's why they assigned her a bed, assigned her a chart.

Lumenical, what she leaves available is her hanging head.

She frozen senseless for the sake of this dawn in the square like just any other place, they totally immersed in Santiago; that woman who has raised her conscious razed head in order to discover her privates after being shaved.

The iridescent one, disturbed, biting the hem of her dress to stretch herself out some time on the bench, apparently finished.

Pale to the end, with her head hanging and her eyes shut, she rests.

So as not to extend her head which could be massaged by experts, examined to the point of tedium, subjected to the point of spasm.

That's the only reason why it would be possible to take the longest rest/ to damage her obscene imaginings/ to stretch out still articulated — white sheets — — odors — on the bench in the square so as to name as remnants her decorated thoughts.

4.3   HER REMNANTS:

Between the years of her birth and death she was able/
to limit herself to three occupations. These being conditioned
by historic events that determined incidents by appearances.

During those years she divided herself between fiction and the
fiction of her occupations. That way she succeeded in striking
a balance among the fiction desired by externals, another she
did not recognize as such and that resulting from both. This
last she designated her own.

From this place her preferences must have been marked,
inscribed in the fiction she worked out concerning everybody
else, although they did not have the plasticity of her desires

She fell into constant errors, disconnecting the dialogues,
redeeming time in scarcely important scenarios. She proposed
aberrant ramblings in language as a means for keeping at bay
any solution by beauty as well as for not sustaining it by any
of its characteristic features. She threw herself into this
unfailing pleasure, recognizing it as being as ephemeral as her
imagination.

It was denied her.
In other people's writing she invigorated her inability to
reinscribe it, in a process equally mistaken.

That was perhaps possible between her years of birth and
death, with the latent alternative of structuring another cycle,
of beginning things in a parallel manner.
                           (files for naming biographies)

Uncultivated sites/ surplus stock/ victims/ human refuse/ open-
air shelters/ assaults.

— You have strange antennae — you changed form or
something?

With all the passivity that characterizes some illuminati, she
lets them examine her with probes so she may be published:
she is consumed, starting from her unordinary thoughts, in a

possible film, with a measured plot.

They cut through her calm reading, the repository of her interior/ as work/ as synthesis/ as reflection/ as defect. Set up as a model she becomes malleable in each one of her fragments so as to disappear later assimilated among objects the square promotes: in every corner/ in its noises/ in some thought overtaken by lassitude.

With probes and bandages over the probes she clings to seclusion.

Disguised and silent, covered with signs, poisoned with sedatives she asked for water because her skin was dried out. It was a little like waking up in the middle of the night, dreaming, with her heart arrhythmic — near the end — and discovering that her head was bandaged and new ideas came into her mind.

In order to disappear afterward blocked from sight, by the cars without managing to cross the path of any gaze/ avoiding the rubbing.

(note on unplowed land)

With open eyes she would peer into the concave hole of those who have not vented their surpluses. Touching her eroticism in the extinguishing of the lights, moaning for what she doesn't have in her insatiable quest for light, just like the pale people who spread their complaints across the landscape that outlines mirages. Hermaphrodites stumble among the pits and protuberances in order to inflict wounds on themselves, maintaining that limit-situation of continuous salivation which could be the metaphor of starshine on damp concrete.

They suck her pieces which do not have the excellence of the original.

Reduced to primitive schemes they are remade translucent in elegances. These delicate bodies susceptible to being pierced

to the pool of their liquids — but without aberrations —
divested of referents, specifying that there's no dreaming in
this electrified solar space. Because behind the trees nothing
has happened and the swamp that arose from her legs was the
penetration of the branches, of the cold that encountered no
protection in its path. Until suddenly the public lighting
suddenly comes on in the square and the lumpen is surprised,
with tears streaming down its face.

(a possible action to be performed during the blinking of the
electric light)

Or maybe she ends up intoning one of those songs they sing
around here.

Expressing the melodrama of those lyrics with facial expressions and sometimes there may surface one of the famous
quotations that break the scheme and she herself may cover
her mouth and start the tragedy over again with voice crystalline, tenuous: with a beautiful voice she sang.

She did it for the cinematography: she stood up/ tested her
voice/ cleared her throat/ tried it again/ did her number/ said
the lyrics in French/ with a miserable accent she did/ praised
and renowned — sheltered by the glitz — with glossy ribbons
on the razed head; an object of jealousy her song, of envy her
dress, an example of daring her gesturing.

She could sway her head back and forth herself in a way never
before imagined, with such subtlety she could do it that no one
would discover her looking for admiration. The naturalness of
this gesture would convince the others of her absolute innocence, of her indifference to the satisfaction of their gazes.
This gesture nobody else in this country could match it, not
this other one either: when she raises one of her hands, she
simply moves it from one of her knees on which she has rested
it, up to clearing the hair from her forehead.

She slowly turns her fingers round and shows raised in the air
the palm that scarcely brushes her nose and cheeks. Only then

does she pass her hand over her head, disordering her hair, raising it shiny.

She notes the look that scans her hand on her pate, the reflection of others' eyes the product of her hair's gleam. But she does it with eyes averted, avoiding the direct crossing, so that this way they can calmly follow her features discovering all their sharp clarity: those strange traces she elaborates when she has lost the gaze.

But she doesn't do that either.

She does not manage to raise the hand completely and the hair she arranges it with a toss of her head. She does not show the hand's curve nor exhibit the palm. She remains with hair flattened down. She lowers her eyes often because she feels the impulse to collide with another gaze that could reveal her in her affectation — in her attempts — because it is she alone who measures in seconds each one of her gestures in this tremendous and wretched production.

But she does it with refinement and almost imperceptibly, because if by chance her gaze crosses the others, she can determine immediately if they will or won't reach the square, if they'll remain there, detecting under the make-up the degrees of paleness borne by their faces.

She lowers her eyes sinking them into the quadrangle where those poor fans find no door ajar.

(component of one of her poses)

4.4   FROM HER FORGETFULNESS PROJECT:

The nails of her toes are to my nails unidentical twins with pinkish stains streaked by white lines.

Her toenails are to my nails twins in the gnawing of their tips.

They too are perfect thick scales as they mark the dimension of the toes that appear again at their edges. To the touch they seem granitic or eroded or diseased if one notes the spots that cross every nail, but each one of these curvatures restores the balance. Her toenails grow wider in accordance with the broadening shape of the toes, but each one of them preserving the preceding margin of flesh. That's why her smallest nails appear like infinitesimal hardnesses that do not protect the toes' flesh in all its magnitude.

Her toenails are to my nails twins in their identical functions, preserving for the touch certain mounds that imply their characterizing forms. Her toenails are to mine twins in keeping at bay fear of the lawn, in obstructing transparency.

Her toenails are to my nails twins in the disorderliness of their cut, in their run-down care. More than finery, her toenails are the element that mediates with the grass, that prevents the dissolution of the flesh of her toes which this way remain fragmentarily protected.

Her toenails are to my nails twins in their absurdity, in being an eyesore, demonstrating that way domestication of the gaze that does not stop to classify their functions.

Her toenails foretell the abandonment of her whole image which has been engraved in the multiple uneven cuts that bound their edges.

Her toenails are just like my nails, crusts.

The toes of her feet are to my toes twins in each joint that provides the mobility necessary for their being shown with the extreme slimness that defines them. This delicacy no doubt begins in their privileged skeletal formation, since despite the natural agglutination of her toes they do not look like discordant parts, keeping instead the definition of their color, which, whitish rose, they retain as a unit.

Her toes are to my toes twins in their texture, not a single blemish on the skin, their lack of erosion distinguishes them as unique and even the natural down ringing them is almost imperceptible except to the touch.

Resting on the ground they spread apart a little and that allows clearer confirmation of the beauty of each one of them in its outline. Her toes are to my toes twins in their sinking into the grass, in that decoration by color where pleasure manifests itself undisguised. That's why the lawn does not hinder the grazing by each one of her toes which tirelessly seek rubbing with the grass.

The soles of her feet are to my soles rough and arched, marked lengthwise by multiple striations that stand out despite the hardened skin that frames them, but in spite of everything they maintain the curve that is measured in their resting on any floor. The soles of her feet are to my soles twins in their concealment and in the resistance, which lessened by the lawn, only there permits deferred rubbing against the earth.

Her eyes are to my eyes sufferers from the gaze, that's why they are the slight nexus that staves off abandonment. My eyes are to her eyes the constant that does not permit mistaking grass for branches.

Elucidating the abandonment, her eyes are to mine the sustenance of the pale people who cross the square and who when no longer in need of her twin eyes will lead their very own to the same irreversible failure.

Her eyes are to my eyes twins in their pigmentation, in the perpetual transparent moistness that protects them. Her eyes generate in my eyes the same twin gaze contaminated by so much of the city of Santiago reduced to grass.

Her eyes are to mine guardians.
Her hands are to my hands twins in their smallness. With

fingers so extremely pointed her nails appear limpid, filtering the rosiness of the flesh which that way accents its curvature.

Each one of her fingers is covered by multiple granulations, intractable lines that become inevitable over each joint which corresponds to the very thickness of the fingers and which mark, finally, the crease separating them from the next one.

Gazed at from the palm, her hands are to my hands sinuous.

Absolutely rose colored her palms are to mine the stage for palmistry and bear no destiny out of keeping with what goes on in the square. Her palms are to my palms the true foundation of pleasure.

Her hands are to mine twins in the absence of gold rings.

Naked, the fingers half open like the sun's rays when electric light does not illuminate the premature darkness in the public square.

Her arms are to mine twins in their symmetry. Perfectly slender they show in the skin's transparency the tracery of veins that encircles them. Covered with down, they assume in the exposure to light a different periphery that is confirmed in the delicacy of her movements cutting the void. Nevertheless, her arms are to mine twins in their failure, their absolute uselessness, in the want of arms that — perhaps — programmed for a fruitful destiny, are denied and they touch the leavings intertwining them with the trees.

Not dependent on benches in the square, her arms are to my arms unaware on the grass, touching as the one and only skin her very own which even in itself avoids the rubbing.

Her arms are exactly like mine sensitive at the wrists so that no sort of life escapes through some hypothetical orifice. The wrists of her arms are for this reason obsessively watched over.

Her waist is to my waist the twin in its wearing away, different in its measurement. In any case irreducible, her waist becomes provocative in demarcating erogenous zones in the balancing that makes room for the torso and the shifting of the thighs. But nobody could find there any form of beauty because her waist is connoted by its amorphousness, nothing about it comforts the gaze or arrests it at that point and in not leading to the flight of imagination, her waist remains like mine unexplored.

Her waist is to mine the twin in its nonexistence.

Her waist is a final point of abandon.

Her waist is the penitentiary/ it is the ecstasy of the end.

Her waist is the twin to mine in its obstinate insistence on this life, it is margination.

Her waist — oh, her waist! — is the twin to mine in its transparency to the soul.

Her soul is material.

Her soul is being established on a bench in the square and choosing as the only true landscape the falsification of this same square.

Her soul is shutting the eyes when thoughts come and reopening them on the grass.

Her soul is this world and nothing else in the lighted square.

Her soul is being E. Luminata and offering herself as another.

Her soul is not being called diamela eltit/ white sheets/ cadaver.

Her soul is to mine the twin.

4.5   That's how her first scene transfers: the camera and
its angle, her thigh in contempt
                              The loony paternalarva surface.
Like that she posed, just like that she posed crack open in
furrows of megalomaniacal sound she joined in the game

pole pelt pes all to curse her name of wild kicks:

what sires? what breed rather is the animal?

what sire?

What name did they inscribe on her?

Thincest works painlessly. It founds and specifies the continuous name, loathsome animal that vouches for its sunken
surface, in the gray of its smeared salival species.

She sweats sediments salts her framework: they wean her
early, mother more ungodly her madonna master for leaving
her on the concrete in the square.
She conceals her womb opens
                    fetus and figure expand in the quadrangle's holes

her father enters moans her ignominious mater
                              her absurd registers imprison her,
they enter her with the force of domination and she takes
charge of her ancient plagiarism. It doubles her, they repeat
her in their yearning, for the surrendered woman who precedes
her.

The male, that indecent colt who inscribes her:
                    her burden of citizenship that she inherits

that flesh incubated in other flesh trembles and lends her
haunch: like larva she snakes into the square +

Thincestress recognizes her breed in his face, the face of the
father, which the face of her father remits to her at the same
time as thaunch her insatiable father'same form.

Animaloid haunched to her wicked matermadona, who raises

her womb on the ground
peeled away by the pater's impulse.
                              snatches the teat from him, that
ample milky part robs him and her hungry muzzle sucks from
the father his product which he gives her in order to perpetuate
her.

the wild mother becomes occlusive and squeezes her teat
delightedly
            the stream spurts
            floods his nape

The milken floods the razed head with sticky liquid that
sleeks.

The father looks after the breed. They measure her genetic
neurons, gamble her in a game of stud: trace those appetites in
her, anal for the mother, the madonna of the anus that cracks +

that way the father son of the mother, in her anal tunnel his
figlio tunnel deposits in order to solidify this likeness.

The surname incestser. The insolence of the proper noun that
the father groans at her in consoling her; darkly they scheme it
when the mater leaves her innards to the preferential paternal
powers + flees from the stigma, the animal loses her distinc-
tive feature; this filly fails but not the haunch that remits her
civic identity card,
only then does he really hauncher
                              when the pater power travels in
the same entrance the well-known mount
            · the patria power that gives her eyes
            eyebrows/ eyelashes/ iris
                        & light
now gives her the spur without bright marks.
Is there any source truer than metal?

Her first scene of the name gets off the track, she throws off
her father's aliases once tested/ th'Argentine one/ thother one
            she includes them in spasms of revolt. She will not
fall again, will not make the front page
her father's face which sinks into her side: multiplies itself,

surpasses the mother's face

                    the victim she shoots up
opens her veins with the needle. Spur's nailed in.
She curses thentrails that double her over. Her mother will not
trot with the burden, the mule will not make it to the stud: the
mulish one incubates only the dry loin the loin razed, can-
kered.
                    fetus and she shifts the larval symptom
more than censuses, she will add his different aliases.

She will donate her vestiges.
                    lawn welcomes her maternally
tree hugs her
                    light unveils her
She has fed herself with the cold milk, she is strengthened by
the male muzzle
    the Scene? the Scene of her atrophied haunch, the take of
her curious orphanhood
Thincest of the theft of her alias/
                    the filth
the dirtiness from all the wallowing that has contaminated her
ancestors and it was more and more, and more they perjured
her until they left her limp in that hole
                    and here we go again the water was being
agitated
and she the fetal filly who gets annoyed
Again they penetrate her?
Not the static square, the perpetual scab that hides her daily
horrors from her. There's no night of her father, fiestaval of
her mother
                    she takes refuge on a hard bed
her cord in its navel course ties her to the bench in the square.
The cord is slender and does not allow her to move, if she
does
it will burst in umbilicancial blood
from the umbilical cord that restrains her, the bitch more than
barking howls.

The bitch stops, she won't be choked to death by her own
umbilical cord
she cuts it/ bleeds/ the bitch has her period.

4.6   The purebred digs in rough with the metal collar at
her neck:
          the leash holds
the leash yanks her when her scent surrenders her to the prey.
If male its smell also lashes her + the tree trunk + the lawn +
the prey flees
          From her bough the maiden falls wounded and
humbles herself folding up her paws. She does not cross and
she is not crossed with
          pack of mutts yapping/ mutt pack
popular serpent of the pack
Her leather cord cinches her throat. She runs round the square,
the square turns finite for her feet
          thimpossible a cinch. Trottin round colludes her with
the lasso, imbricates her with the leather.
          And she cuts, wants to cut with her canine the
cowhide already cured. She sharpens her fang to flee from the
thick trunk that clasps her claw
          she digs holes herself to block up her redoubts
the pedigreed bitch is chased by the mutts. The bitch's mange
gets better
          thinflammation of the bitch/ thinfection of those
mutts
What point bringin her the leash? what kinship's claimed?
what kindness
          does her bark exude?
The purebred gets it on with the mutts?
worked so meticulously her slim leash, so wrought the
harness-maker's craft shows: collar for the bitch/ owna for
her/ master/
          Trumpet snout or boss for the bitch
her guardian who protects her from those mutts followin her.
Who pulls off the pack. On her scent comes and howls the
wild mongrel pack barks at the pampered bitch
          bitch scarcely pampered on the leather leash, bitch
that without a collar, libertine species would find herself in
kinship with the mutts: she'd do it?
          the bitch would crack her scent?
the collar impressed on her it's not leather, metal spikes,
          painless if she reins in
but not if she ran. Her ownas implacable
this bitch's master — if she had one — why provoke her in

that square that doesn't slam the door on the mutt pack +
     the cross between them it's obvious they're pure
gutterunnin, the crumblin inside the square.

     They eat the remains
but instead the bitch perversely sniffs this food
     her scent drags on the concrete, her pointy muzzle/
her pink doggy tongue in the lickin
let the others tongue her so's the leash and its ferrous points
sink into her throat
     the bitch stops short
            scares
the mutt pack that same bitch does so's to break from the
noose
           the complaint changes or somethin?
     barks, sounds that resemble
     reedy quena or brassy trutruca, the mutt pack
decorates, punctures, conquers, circles/ curing in machitú
dancing
     collar of silver round her neck
forehead in silver
     metallic ankles in silver
     leather-soled sandals
animal hide the feet as well
     Machi
the mater healer towers up for the mutts
     trumpets for the dogs
muzzle for the animals
               muzzle as well for this bitch
                    sounds
                  of reunion

The cacique Toqui tocsin tocatta in pure silver hides her
     her muzzle her cheekbones
the almond eyes
     they dance her in circles now those crossbreeds. The
breed

the breed towers without the privilege of other breeds
     the languid sound comes forth
the square is dotted. The Altiplanar space refers

to itself and to the bitch
they loosen her collar/ let her lose the silver
her breast's lectrified the thatched ruka topples
the bitch surrenders her silver collar
the Toqui to the owna/ to the master to the trumpeter
dances his trutruca in fiestaval
also mastered the bitch dances
the mutt bitch
without the silver collar
so why's she strayin?

5

Quo Vadis?

5.1   Quo vadis mafiosa so her parted mane will fall once
and for all. She'll play maybe rouletted just in the head,
digging up mask after mask and a fallen word she will be:
letter modulated on the grass, she'll rub body and lawn,
tongue and lawn, leg and lawn and the liquid.

From reiteration she will raise up her gaze.

No cinematic situation now but narrative, ambiguous, erring.

She could have said, for example:
this square's run down, full of patchy lawn. My legs no longer
shine when I rub them, nor do the hairs stand up on end, this
down that subtly covers my legs. I no longer like dragging
myself around here under the streetlamp whose peeling infects
me. Because my legs instead get covered with dirt and then
I'm not aware of the pricking up of the hairs that run through
me, oh yes, they penetrate me.

But this is how she constructs her first scene, because she
continues dragging herself along in order to get rid of the mud
stuck to her skin and with all the touching the grazing is
produced. She moves muscles slowly, holds them back at each
contraction. What's the point saying it: she's under the
streetlight. She's under the streetlight in the square and
although the cold spreads along here she stretches out on the
grass to sleep. But sleep won't come and she tosses and turns
to find a different position. She tries keeping her eyes shut all
the time so as not to scare sleep away. She is an image totally
different for the one reading her. She rolls round on the grass
crossed by her stubborn insomnia. She stretches out all the
way. From far away she is a sheet spread out on the grass,
from close up she is an open woman, farther away she is grass,
from farther still she is nothing. It's so dark in the square.
From the sidewalk opposite it's an illuminated quadrangle.

Like a zoom, that's writing. The woman who sleeps or wants
to sleep reappears, but that's not how it is: it's the pleasure of
spreading out playing, with the delight in her own image.
Infantile stretching's what it is. Like a trickster she does it.
Because playing at distorting the gaze with lack of light, that
trick's been worked to death. She conquers this way the

ambiguous, confusion mounts and insomnia is a fleeting fact. All this movement's only for succeeding at rubbing one of her legs on the grass and that's why she feigns not being able to sleep, as if her mind encompassed nothing but this state.

She turns over, hopeless on her bed, but her awareness is focused on her leg's every grazing of the grass, that extreme moment when her down bristles up, rising from the leg and creating another circuit of proximity.

She keeps her eyes closed. She moves imperceptibly until ceasing to move at all.

She does not move because the first rain falls on the square.

She will not sleep, nor will she be able to enjoy with her legs, the personal luminous nap of her down.

The rain falls in heavy drops and she gets up from the lawn in order to take shelter under the trees. The cold has diminished considerably, replaced by the discomfort of the water that begins to open striations in the ground covered with grass.

The gray dress is penetrated and rain trickles over her flesh: the back, the breast, the legs. Nothing predisposed to this soaking, maybe on account of not looking at the sky, maybe on account of that.

She trembles on seeing the shimmering of the concrete squares which begin to glisten from the effect of the streetlights. In contrast she instead is diluted in opacity. With body weighed down by all the water her gray wool dress absorbs. It's a dead weight that drags at each one of her steps; the dress is a burden getting darker and darker, by contrast the square appears in good light, enlarged, dazzling.

And not her, it's that dress that deprives her of her atavistic beauty, more than the rain which in itself is only an additive per se. She erred. She chose her closest decoration badly. Once again she worked like an amateur. Consequently she plays at losing this scene. She remains rigid waiting for the last of the water that does not stop, just the opposite, it falls even harder.

Her body stumbles. It is her structure that is close to falling. The square has surpassed her. She is on the brink of losing her armature, rig, she was no decoration for the square but just the reverse: the square was her page, only that. But her face convulsed now, her razed head wet, her body gaunt which makes for the one reading her a streak of tree, waste.

She reflects, her eyes travel over her dress, she cleans the water off her face. She looks around her and notes that not a single pale one has arrived tonight and even though there's still time, she intuits that they will not come, as if the show she was going to offer them no longer made any sense. She is alone and that's why her performance is solely for the one who reads it, who takes part in her self-same solitude.

They will come gaze to gaze, thoughts will face off and that's the only reason why it will be necessary to invent the pleasure that has been avoided.

She comes out from under the tree and is inundated by rain, says — I'm thirsty — but obstinately seals her lips, makes way for the hallucination, tenses her hand from fear.

She has assumed the rhetoric of riddles, plunged into the everydayness of this situation she climbed into the indescribable. She imagined herself: with neons, gold rings, earrings. Squared by fetishes she returned to the letter traced by a shining silk glove — entirely significant — she interrogates herself in poetic, figurative language. She breaks her model, erects herself into chapter.

She starts saying every beautiful word until going into ecstasies, smiling she says them and so this landscape is changed into day for night and although her eyelids are pierced, she convinces herself not to look so as not to be touched by the streak.

From wool into silk, from flesh into mannikin, until the rain slides over this new support. So it's no longer necessary that she say anything more or call herself precious stone, solid material, in order to be able, maybe, to bask in that water that in penetrating her does not touch her.

That's how she was transfigured in body by calling upon her finery, attaining perfection for herself. But she got rid of it, opting for her gray wool and still she went on shining calligraphically with equal brio.

She simply denies herself the contemplation of the pale people so as to exhaust in herself the appeal of the contemplated.

No one previously had investigated her the way she did herself faced with that unforeseeable rain.

With the most significant of cautions she hits her limit which is the passage of the night, so as to say to herself maybe — gold ring — and the fiction was stripped away in which all her defenses were knocked down. Without reflectors of any sort, she rehearses.

Passed along from image to word, by means of special effects she turns to twisting language, mounting it emotionally. She does over, correcting the matrixes now ready for reproduction.

It will be printed with conscious errata sought in the cracks of the concrete squares where the shreds of each scene are contained. The reading of the foot prints' mark in the subtle differences of color that only the rain succeeds in bringing to light.

Every one of these signs is decipherable for her. She would be able to weave that way innumerable yarns just by untangling the web of her gray wool dress. Unraveling this strand in order to extend it as writing in the square. Reweaving by chaneling its coloring, gray over the gray of the ground may tempt her. She touches the dampness of the dress and feels the slipperiness of the concrete squares. To rise up into the trees and breaking the branches, complete the novel with them.

Transforming each one of those materials, marking the pauses with neons, the titles with flourescents, breaking the sterility of the rains until summoning by spectacle the pale people who will order a possible reading, revising some texts, deleting others, keeping the batteries at their peak: all this electric light that opposes the rain.

It is raining in the square. But she has spread a plastic sheet over the stone bench and covers herself. The drops echo slippery on her body. She does not feel cold and is even sweating from the emanation of the plastic that encloses her. She watches the square. She arises still covered and on each of the benches she leaves plastic sheets in preparation for the arrival of the pale people. This is no unheard-of show for her, because rain always falls again after the intense chills that pierce them during the nights.

She covers herself again with the plastic, remains motionless amid the heavy drops, until one leg moves, rubbing hard against the other and once again her raised down answers to her whim: even under rain that leg of hers drags:

Her pubic hair on their buttocks that frenetic posteriority the rubbing.

The pale people exiting and entering day in and day out salivish, falling out of the hubbub: she did not achieve displeasure.

She did not achieve it, because the contrivance that extruded iridescent colors was so distant from her that it dragged her to consummation.

She didn't achieve displeasure because her legs gave out.

She didn't achieve displeasure because entirely beautiful she rubbed her breast.

She didn't achieve displeasure in the interweaving of her hairs, on the inner sides of those same legs there remained mobile particles.

These same particles at her gaping lips.

Along with the coquetry of her open legs: the eyelids and the awareness of a solid body — her own — which suited to different situations was able to acquire a special autonomy, denying itself to rigorousness. But she escaped. Those same legs convulsed by pubic hair, particles generating gape, generously avoiding displeasure.

But how did those shot pale ones remain all these hours with
their gaze at a loss, during that private moment, detached from
the contamination of all other thought, leaving those other legs
empty, moist, downy, moistened on the inner sides with the
sphincter contracted. The shut legs of those poor jutting
breasts obtaining-consummating displeasure, signaling the
need for reconstructing their legs in the closeness of the
rubbing, in the unique fleeciness which phantasmagoric
repeats the solitary action. Doubly beautiful in the rubbing
which in spite of being imaginary is the causal liquid.

And the pale people yes indeed they know how to bump their
pubic fleece on the frontal fleece pubical: rubbing.

Her pubic fleece on the fleecy pubis plus her two legs crossed
to the rhythm of the hips, imagining the rubbing.

Take notice of her pubic fleece in the face the rubbing up:
forehead, eyes, cheeks and the whole retracted jaw.

Her pubic fleece on the torso the rubbing: spasms in the
shoulders, neck, arms, waist. And her withered breasts, what
about them?

Her pubic fleece ascendant, the mouth the rubbing: the teeth,
the tongue. Anyone can get disgusted by saliva. Quit it.

Her pubic fleece in her hands, the intense stupid rubbing, but
fingers and fingernails beyond wildest dreams.

Her hairs displaced from her side and this leg of hers crossed
in empty air, raised wearily toward the edges. This same tired
leg of hers seeking renal relief, her grace note, with all her
might held up toward the border's weak emptiness that does
not contain the dampness necessary for the side, which ought
to be pierced by the wetness of the hairs. That extenuated leg
drawn up toward the buttock seeking in the other posteriority
covering for her radiant fleece, until the half-open thighs may
offer another sort of stain.

The yielding of the leg that did not grant her displeasure
because distant from herself she rubbed her breast, while her
hands activated by the violence of her damp fleece stuck
stubbornly to the sides of her thighs, they wove mobile
particles.

These same particles at her gaping lips programming the ritual
coquetry of the open legs, the oscillating eyelids in the body
that's messed up by all this sweat and that way who can put up
with displeasure that doesn't have the firmness of fingers, Jane
Doe with the lost gaze.

— But I myself I lent my legs, vacant, pubic, downy, my poor
lapidated legs and that way my own true name leaped out at
me when that pubic fleece mounted my buttocks, calling
myself light, which was so heavy on her head that I named her
the mother with her fleece at my hip, at the afflicted kidney,
tirelessly in search of rubbing —

I insist: in search of rubbing — those pale people — who in
mere automatism take their name from the buttocks' posture,
until the streetlights' coming on shows the trees in the
reinscription of terror. But up to that moment the body is
parceled into different autonomies, whose axis is centered on
the dampness of the fleece.

And truly it was delicious the rubbing of those pale people
who, nevertheless, directed their gazes toward other Chilean
landscapes.

And tell me now what you feel stretched out on the bench,
covered with plastic, back fully turned on literature. Because
like that a person can say anything whatsoever — tell me
something about your arrogance — you can verify how those
pale people started arriving at the remaining benches and each
one covers up, though already pierced under the rain and they
then find their gazes distorted, ambiguous on the square. Their
gazes — I mean — that are projected though the polyethylene
producing a distorted angle, transforming the streetlamps, the
trees, the lawn, until they eventually locate her — one more
deformed bundle — she the one who moves in the impunity of
rubbing. That's how the rain is unleashed on them but she rubs

herself inside the plastic, shutting out the carnal pleasure of that water.

— But those others how they shine, how they endure their mastery by folds, how they regard and greet each other unleashed, pubic, clean. Knowing their skin bristles up from the water that does not touch them. Yes, their legs and hairs along with the mouth transmit actions: tongue on lips, eyes misty under the plastic and the streetlamps are turned on for nobody, for nobody at all this decoration. They arrange themselves like lines ordered on the page and every inch of the square imprints them and every drop of the rain inks them. They are printed and stretched taut in their very movement and by rubbing they are published: familiar in their order, typecast —

— What an uprising of the lumpenpack at that tolling: Illusionism of the plastic that negates them in fragmentary modules, reiterating them like splinters, current posters or placards maybe, leaping out of the cracks, executed like graffiti: their bodies —

— How they smuggle their gazes, preceding into the dive-like square, fugitives from the printed word, scarcely rough drafts, handwriting, coarse terminology impeach them. But neither are we about to say that this is the dregs. Not at all: the construction of a transitory narrative that takes as its model a ragged bag lady. She spread her proclamation in flyers, those same words also produced a ruled floor on the square's cement —

— They shine whole, their desires for fiction like orifices, by atomizing themselves in electricity which is returned on the other side of the page distempered by readings: that's how they lose their blotches and regain the old color, where their feet are not bandaged their legs not ulcerated. The entire lost cadaster umbilical in its insignificance. Writing piled up on posters, this unbridled proclamation of the square —
— So as to be read from behind the plastic sheets protecting them from the rain and that's why deciphered like that, gaze and text, body and mind are rubbed together. That's how the novel opens, the characters appear, they are read under the

square's light. The plastic prevents deterioration, like a sleeve, like a book jacket. The pupil adjusts itself and the streams of rain enjoy falling on skin —

But no: they mark the concrete, feed the trees, defy the electricity.

"Without life along the way — except for the reference to the desired stereotype — they have hidden glitz-Chile by blotting them out, in order to enjoy themselves decked out like caricatures, those very same ones who reach their plenitude under the plastic that deprives them of achievements that treacherously destroy them. In literature they have done it."

"Because throughout this loathsome territory they have been selected for disembodiment by being transported via writing, in the stupid procedure that does not reveal their aura to them, blocking their possibility of growing pale and reappearing under the electric light which alone can show their garish blotches."

"Wrung out and printed they have been denied that light so as to compose perfectly false illustrations — without risks — that image which allows them intermittencies, the deluded distance of the person who has believed in a kind of deferred permanence."

"No literature has portrayed them in all their immeasurability, that's why they, as daily labor, cling to their shapes and every gesture when they touch each other leads to climax. That's how they come close to finishing, pleasure being that threshold: pure aberrant rambling that rain."

"Knowing that no literature has sketched them, definitely bored they pose. The successive angles to which they expose themselves transmit them bidimensional in the single, precarious certainty that nobody embraces in the containment of writing. But it's more than that, they fold down to lifesize by sticking those words on their body: they sweat under the plastic."

Nevertheless rain begins to fall on the square and the cold

drops in intensity. The pale people cluster around E. Luminata. They are drenched, they cover their head with newspapers, go take shelter under the trees. Their feet sink into the ground until they are completely bogged in mud. For the first time their images decline, even she, with the wet razed head, she presents a desolate appearance herself. Like a screen, the rain is perceptible through the lamplight. Water runs down their faces, diminishes their figures, renders them opaque. There are no roofs over their heads save for the trees' sparse foliage.

They'll be wet like that, surprised and perhaps they will commiserate among themselves and understanding the fragility of their bodies, will again curse the square's defect.

They do not move, their thoughts stay on their own track unrelated to any incident. They lose themselves in fictions, investigate their situation. No actions are possible beyond their own tongue which, even in the favorable surroundings, does not come out. They know their dialogue would trivialize the dismembering by observation, besides they know beforehand what they would allude to. It is already written.

They hurled their proclamations when she took from her bag the piece of plastic which, being insufficient, she crumpled between her hands and flung to the ground.

The plastic, the plastic was one of her many illusions.

5.2   If the spotlight illuminated her razed head, she
would part with her own hands that diminished hair. Would
show the illuminated skull.

if the foot were illuminated by the spotlight/
if the foot were illuminated by the spotlight, it would give it
free time only to graze, to grow disturbed, to become one with
the grass.

if on the flank the spotlight
were to illuminate, if the flank by the spotlight were illuminated it would absorb her pimpled hide, nobody coolly puts up
with a spotlight on the flanks.

but if it fell on her shoulders
the innumerable curves of her column would be searched by
the spotlight.

the thigh, scarcely a fragment of her thigh
raised, erecting itself fleeing would be apprehended by the
spotlight, even if nobody knew it was her thigh.

the shoulder, if that spotlight points at the articulation
a move of her arm could put the shoulder in movement, the
shoulder could be covered by the hand, that obstacle could be
raised to the spotlight.

Otherwise
if a lumperratic order the spotlight illuminated, she would lose
immediately her razed head, her foot, her flank, her back, her
shoulder, her whole focus, all her work.

Coming into the spotlight/ the scene
if it's a matter of moaning, she moans in a prolonged, annoying way, fine moaning if it's moaning they want from her/ the
tip of her chin trembles to be convincing/ she copies all the
expressions of moaning — in order to dupe them — lips fallen
eyes half-closed: if the trek the scene she wanted to control, to
the point of dragging herself she would prolong it, the
plodding pace, the weight of her feet
                    she would hurt the soles of her feet just to get this
                    scene right, naked the soles of her feet, the garment,

the veil, the thick medallion, the cupola, the mantle,
the jingling bells around the ankles, the tambourines
in hand, the silk, the golden threads, the vermilion on
the cheeks, the beauty marks painted on her forehead,
the red mouth, the crown of thorns, the white teeth,
the laurel, the mulish haunch, the dancer, the ocular
ruler, the spy, the injured woman, the victim, the
libidinous old hag, the courtesan, the woman muffled
in gauze, the chansonnière, the innocent girl, the
forsaken woman: she would moan all the poses at
once, would walk copying the scenes.

If for film or photo on the bench in the square they shot her,
she would give good account of herself as the lovers, would
put on her sweet expression seated on the green of a bench/
    the old woman in her would take up her knitting
    the old man in her would read
    the boy with his ball to the lens a smile would send,
    the woman awaiting her wish, gazing toward the
    edges of the square
    the man suffering from hardships whom she bears
    the man persecuted in her
    the lost woman she is.

If by snapshot the camera lens courted her, she would play the
gesture of the hand upon the knee/
                                        a fall,
catching any object whatsoever in her hand, smiling, laughing
uncontrollably, being seated negligently on a stone bench,
hidden in profile by a tree, settling her skirts after a sudden
gust, covering her head with a newspaper, the whole all-too-
familiar naturalness.

If the soundman recorded her, if he tried to render her voice:
    she would say entire speeches — emphasis and
indifference — submissive tones, intemperate shouts, terror
perhaps, enmity or that happy meeting, all the closing lines/
she would give the soundman the last seconds of the scene:
death of the heroine.

But if she herself were the reading, she would be imprinted on
the reader in letters/ she would achieve linear efficacy,
nuanced history, headings, she would traverse all the typography, papers of various weights, latest model press, all for the
reader who reads her, in writing she would even get so far as
foreign language:

English, French, Provençal alphabet or of the
disdained Aymará, Mapuche, to please the dominators, she
would be written in dialects, Greek characters for erudition,
the Arabic language/ exotic Quechua for the slave/ Spanish/

Over thresholds would pass genres chivalric/ pastoral/
picaresque/ serial/ troubadour/ bourgeois drama/ pamphlet/
tragedy and comedy/ experimental try-out/ hand written/
letterpress/ bookshelf, library, reading aloud, recitations,
speeches, proclamations/

graffiti
if the spotlight picks her out, the camera, the sound, the reader,
the plots, all that marked fiction/

If the spotlight, if the spotlight went out, the plot would really
begin.

5.3   On the square the rain has left dampness pierced by
that special odor emanating from the earth. This other night
still does not clear. The cloud cover is visible by the light of
the streetlamps.

Damp earth and the cold grows. It's always like that after rain
and decides the extreme melancholy that changes the square
into a unique, uninhabited object. Any walk there will be
tinged with loneliness, an image of hopelessness or desertion
being projected, like stage tricks in fiction.

She is lost, pale and shivering, still wet from the night before.
She is sick or falling sick rather from being in this state. Cast
to the edge of sterility she has few remaining projections.

Those pale people are there, it's true, but they are not interested in her deprivations, as if their private stories were
disengaged from these images. The lumpen put up only the
façade so as to distribute themselves selectively along it, like
decoration, like fantasies. But from being there all that time
and their gaze being exchanged — in spite of herself — their
looks collide. Convulsed by the cold her gaze seeks them first
in a casual way, then investigates, finally her gaze comes to
rest on them. But afterward it shuns them again in order to
forestall the catastrophe, she takes comfort among the others
who follow her and though witnesses to her reduction, she is
always going to outdo them in her glitter.

That's why she doesn't let herself go all the way in contemplation, though the others may recognize the effort it costs her.

Conquering the abyss. Concealing the possibility.

Nor are they just somebodies or other who can go around
Santiago begging. Not at all. Always keeping in mind their
professional performance and that speeding they confirm
themselves in their filming. And although they might beg
along these busy streets, the city is outside, as everyday
activity: mock rehearsals, paid work.

But if she grazed her gaze a little more against the other and
let it go so far that its black against the black eye was rubbed,

then vulgarity would be the written form. That sentimental mania, her trivial emotionality.

She sacrifices the gaze, castrates herself of the eye that gazes at her to the point of wearing it down and renewing it in its true role.

Wet she repeats her pose against the tree and takes hold of it with her two hands — making an effort so that her cheeks will be tinted with a little color —

Initiated into vertigo she has let her gaze change into mere surface and empty she tries to regain her vigor. Discarded and drenched that way she had the clearest of her hallucinations: she saw beauty descended in its particular somatic dimension, in the very description of her fallen eye. Fetish of her dress and her hidden breasts, incorrigible in her form read by veracity, subversive by nature. I mean, she saw her beauty/ examined herself in her finiteness until those others turned so irreverently perfect that they made choice impossible for her.

Although frozen stiff they do not come to gnawing the square's dust because their voices are swapped for writings and once more the press falls and a pink tone — her cheek — marks the error of the ink that infiltrated letter with letter on opposite pages. But the lumpenpack does not stop its machines, up at dawn and awake all night they come back to the matrixes, re-examine them under the square's light. They take pleasure in their avatars, redoing the plates which defective serve as other material. Nothing goes to waste and although the downpour has devastated them they rush out more energetically, taking precautions, learning these jobs. They get ready to shine once published and insomnia may then be nothing more than a thing of the past.

She has neutralized her gaze, recomposing herself out of the fleeting weakness of hanging on those eyes that offered the fiction of a bad bet. She has regained color and pose. She makes the most of the wet razed head, of the incipient wrinkles and works up her customary smile.

Works up her smile because she sees them only in their

commercial, transferable product. Circulating material abused by the foreignness of the square's alien eye which may not know about the damaged originals, the scrapping of the matrixes, which will not hold up to their second printing.

She bends over with her head between her knees and with her hands bristles up her hair. Brings out her natural smile. Cleans her teeth with her tongue: the concrete will pick up the image. Cheeks tinted she stops under the lamp and on the metal her finger writes in imaginary calligraphy — like kids — WHERE YOU GOING and with her whole hand completely rubs out the writing.

She tries it again in the center of the square, curved over the cement, occupying ample spaces with her letters.

She practices her words. The others observe her from their places. Time after time until the hand reddens and is skinned from all the rubbing out.

Finally she gets up and her gesture shows that she is ready and one of the pale people reaches out a piece of chalk to her. Almost dragging herself over the ground, she begins to construct large letters that take up the entire center of the square. Gone across and the —where you going — allows her a new arrangement.

The square's tinsel is titled. Lamps and cables, grass and ground, benches of wood and benches of stone: everything's organized.

Pleased with the discovery, the pale people make the effort to read from every possible point. They keep their vertiginosity moving, they flatten out and raise up letters according to their location. She seats herself on the bench in the square to watch them. Reads their writing, approving everything. Her hand clenches the chalk and pieces of it disintegrate beneath her fingers. The crumbs fall onto the concrete but she doesn't see that, attentive as she is to the approving movement of the lumpen.

She has lost her impassivity and now her heart is agitated by the desire to measure the strength of the lines, she knows she has introduced a break in her attitudes and that's exactly why she hopes that the fit of enthusiasm will pass, so those others may really begin to read and then catalogue the action.

Let them get involved with the legend.

They, in turn, begin halting their movements. Their lips murmur the phrase, coming closer and closer to the words, some even tread on them. Finally they cover them completely with their feet. They remain rigid on top. That way nothing is written on the ground, they continue as protagonists occupying the cement. It's obvious that they feel expelled to the edges of the square like notes in the margin. That's why they cover up the lines. They have understood the aggression.

They do not look at her and slowly their feet rub against the ground. As in an improvised dance, their rhythms rub out the chalk, destroy her title. They move off. A gray stain spreads over the center of the square, gone are the letters.

She rises from the bench and approaches them. She bends and with her hands keeps dispersing the traces, centimeter by centimeter, hole by hole.

Everything's not cleaned away, but the whiteness of the chalk almost disappears. The lumpen pull back until they are lost amid the trees' shadows. Still dragging against the concrete pavement she again begins drawing letters with her fingers. She does it again and again until finally, grasping firmly the bit of chalk she writes her phrase in even bigger dimensions, leaving large blanks between letters. It appears — where you going — in faultless calligraphy, without so much as a waver from the handwork.

She remains there, stopped alongside a letter. She begins her trek among the letters, taking care not to step on them. She reviews them one by one before turning her eyes to the pale people who watch her from the darkness. She knows beyond a shadow of a doubt where each one of them is and although her eyes do not distinguish them, she is aware that they will indeed receive her gaze. They do not come out and she keeps on looking at them until her eyes are worn out by fatigue. She turns, her hands fall, her head falls as well. She understands.

She patiently goes back down on her knees on the ground and with the hem of her dress begins to rub out the writing, calmly, methodically, meek.

They then emerge, come out in numbers and with their feet confirm the rubbing out. Once more they are occupying their space in a new labor.

They take their time in order to do a good job, although clearly, the cleaning will not be completed until many other footsteps carry off the minuscule bits of chalk among footfalls.

She rises and looks at them: going up to them she hands each one a bit of the chalk she is breaking between her fingers. With lowered head she does it and they receive it the same way, but taking care not to rub it.

Only the very tips of their fingers touch the bit of chalk.

Now it is she who is lost in the depths of the trees.

Each one controlled by her vision.

She smiles, making her characteristic grimace. She has won.

They seat themselves on the benches around the center. Head between hands, shoulders drooped, they are beauties. She, meanwhile, has leaned her back against the trees and remains erect from head to foot, yearning.

She spies on their movements, knowing that this one will raise his head and open his hand in order to look at the chalk between his fingers and then search for her in the darkness, knowing what she is waiting for, until her illuminated grimace reaches the center of the square and their faces are exposed.

This lumpenpack pretend-writes and rubs out, parcels out the words, the fragments of letters, they rub out their supposed errors, try out their calligraphies, steady the shaking, agree to the printing.

They stay still watching and like professionals begin to lay out their own lines in the center. It's perfect. They get carried away on the slope of the letter, made literate, corrupted by printing.

So well distributed in their spaces that the line is left free so another may continue it. She can begin to read from there. But instead she stops at the tops of the letters. Her eyes measure the lines and travel to the tired bodies that drag themselves for her in the square and mute allow the thought to come together.

They finish but still they do not get up all the way. They again search for her in the darkness that shelters her. They detect her and fling the remains of the chalk into the grass. They go toward the benches and leave her the site of the reading and at last the "where you going" is she herself in the center of the square, bathed in paleness, thoroughly dried off.

She is the same ragged bag lady who stretches herself over the letter and the floor's dampness is nothing compared to the magnificence of her length upon the ground, with the same dampness of the gray dress and the razed head. She has received her best attributes, wet she had to be, sick from the cold, weary. For the first time her smile convulses her/she has seen the complete phrase and she drags herself over it for the rubbing, the dampened dress is imprinted, even the emaciated face is imprinted.

Because the hard concrete that lacerates her back doesn't matter to her, since as a gambler she has won anyway, conquering the coarseness, adding another dimension to the overbearingness of her presence.

Ink was that downpour that has negotiated the perfect gray of her dress.

She cannot stop now, so renewed and so perfect in her paleness that for the first time she could bring her face toward them, in order for them to take pleasure in her skin and perhaps she could even allow them to measure her with the tip of their fingers, the same fingers that pretend-wrote their millimetered lines.

In order that those inked fingers could draw her whole, stamp her indelible trace and that way the square's fleeting lines would fall into a series upon itself and she herself would show up at the benches, the trees, the lamps, the lawn, that whole square finally could store up the ink to repeat other writings.

6

6.1   Imagine a square space, constructed, enclosed by trees: with benches, lights, lighting cables, the concrete surface paved in squares and in patches the ground covered with grass.

Imagine this space contained within the city.

Imagine this city space at nightfall with its parts shrouded in dusk, though still clear.

Imagine this space desolate.

Imagine this desolate space just when the electric light comes on: the beams cast over its surface.

Imagine the entire square space illuminated by different beams filtering through the trees.

Imagine there any figure seated on a bench with eyes closed.

Imagine that figure seated on the bench with eyes closed and the cold spreading fiercely, unleashed.

Imagine that this figure is a woman with eyes closed, huddled against the cold, alone in the square.

Imagine that this woman is a ragged bag lady in the square, gone numb with cold.

Imagine her feet crossed on the ground and her head buried against her breast, hiding her face, with her eyes closed.

Imagine the trees tossed by the wind revealing the lighting cables and in their midst that woman.

Imagine the city still, silent, only the night passing.

Imagine the woman seated on the bench with her eyes closed under a light.

Imagine the light on the woman's head.

Imagine a powerful light on the woman's bowed head.

Imagine her hand illuminated on the bench in the square.

Imagine her feet illuminated, curved on the ground.

Imagine the curvature of her back.

Imagine her curved.

Imagine her in other circular gestures.

Imagine her shut in.

Imagine the woman with her head lowered to avoid a light.

Imagine her completely curved body illuminated by a powerful light.

Imagine her head illuminated.

Imagine the nape of her neck shining illuminated.

Imagine the illumination of her closed eyes.

Imagine her fingernails illuminated on the bench.

Imagine her replaced under the light by another curved figure.

Imagine the scene constituted by a powerful light.
Imagine everything in tatters under that light.
Imagine her own rags exposed to a powerful light.
Imagine the imprinting under a light.
Imagine the extreme curvature imprinted under a light.
Imagine the extreme curvature imprinted under a powerful light.
Imagine the illumination of every electric light.

6.2   THE GRAFFITI IN THE SQUARE

Writing as proclamation.

Santiago de Chile which appeared by deceptive
means and with errata they've deleted
constructions from it and that's why the
pale people prod it as they prod you who thought yourself
protected. They are beyond urban
measurements, in a different situation, that's exactly why
beauty wound up tumbling to the ground. A bit as though
the sun would have ended up
excluding them.
But still those people discourse on other
foundations, something impossible to understand
fully, because the places wherein
they are proposed derive from the most primal, from the
disintelligence of the person who knows
concrete in only one of its aspects.

She wrote:
like the most cracked of madonnas I lent him my body
stretched out in the square so he'd lick it.

Writing as folly.

They arrived/opened holes in the ground in order
to construct their buildings.
They had strength of spirit that people hereabouts, astonished
aimed for. Poor people in rags — lumpen —
longing for that strength they weren't able to find
because their immutable expressions inhibited us
and so, faces raised up, we spent a
lifetime until they threw us away.
They weren't contemplating us since this limited
thought did not illumine the glistening dust jacket
of the divine. Each building bordered the hole
like a trimmed tree.
The beauty of the concrete gave rise to the presumption of
drowsiness.

She wrote:
stretched out on the lawn I told you all the beautiful words,
madonna, so you wouldn't stop, madonna I told you beaming.

Writing as fiction.

In everything oneiric, permanently
distanced we can accede
surprised to celebrations. Bursting
onto the foreseeable front page like
façades in this disorder that
implicates work completed by the one who
receives honors which he gets on
loan for holes that others have
left. And so we show up
illuminated by electric light to found
with our personal presence the bandage
and wounds, perhaps shrunk from carnality
we raise faces on this landscape
to just then
confront these edifices that
gleam in full autonomy.

She wrote:
I get wet in pure torment, yes madonna, I get drenched.

Writing as seduction.

A balanced mix emerging serially
from a subterranean cavity. Incidental
height that crashes to the ground so as to
start decorating all the unveiled
space and that way compel eyes
that had not desired the portent,
had not even longed for
anything, toward the ill-fated participation
of the sacreds in this kind of dragging
by light.
Habitable buildings in precise diameters.
That's what they offered. And that's why, when
we sank our hand into the earth repulsion
struck us on the head, just as indicated in
the ancient chronicles that hang from the
constructions and did not offer
total security.

She wrote:
crack me with branches madonna, inflame me with leaves.

Writing as meshing gears.

Impediments and errors turned up.
Their craving exteriorized in such a way
that surprise left us soulsick,
but even so the fact went beyond language.
How many doubts were indicated — the enigma
remained — with us trembling slightly
and chained to the spirits of the portents.
But it wasn't known that their youthfulness
was a deception thrust in our face
tarnished by lack of brightness, that we didn't
rely on their make-up/ their gifts/
we didn't budge. It was a matter of
following along by dint of transformations
over uneven and enclosed ground.

She wrote:
she besmirches me this madonna in rags, stains me.

Writing as sentencing.

The heroes change into traces to be
followed amid the cables with strange
symbologies, legends almost. Without asking
anyone's opinion frosted we came
to pierce eyes, repeating archetypical poses
but unawares.
The era of foundations was the dense
blockage by underground passages that invited
cardinal effort/ cardinal points
gazing at the light that filtered in adding
yet another specter to the concept of beauty,
so as to ratify the notion of aesthetic change
by the greatest number of passages to the interior
of thought. The seasons did not
disappear as specific forms. Rather
they turned brief for the buildings which
absolutely sparkled. Paradisiacal
wrappings that confounded everyone in
the multiplicity of their hysteria.

She wrote:
send me to that other man madonna, oh yes send me at once to
all the others.

Writing as rubbing.

Then everything stayed inside. We remained
embedded in these new respirations,
with the fine dust deposited by the
laceration, without configuring
by any means negative signs, without
configuring anything actually. The heaps
anticipated systems of communication, through the
vents of these shelves. Everything converged
on the buildings — mind — body — steps
fixed the course. We came to be homogeneous
in the end, but distant and voiceless. Signs
illumine heads and order the filling of the
constructions which return to their original state:
wastelands.
That's how systems were created that required
rapid implementation. Transformed
one into another we looked at the city that
in itself didn't resemble anything important, but
once placed in life we needed
to stretch out on its platform.

She wrote:
drag me to the water madonna, find me the spout.

Writing as evasion.

Unhealthily pale — prowling—
packed with fear they remain in the
hope of controlling the chaos of the
foundation. With their eyes illuminated by
extensive light we fix on an objective.
We understand properly that all this calamity
owes its consistency to the approximate irradiation
of meaning.
But them, condemned, they keep insisting on our
searching and Santiago becomes blurred by chimeras.
There's not much left to construct and that's why
our senses are transfigured so as to hold on to
that slight glimpse of understanding which endures.
Intensely pale myself I bedeck myself
heavily painted to reflect myself in those holes,
multiplied by cerebral stimuli that
situate me at the edge of an abyss that
will irredeemably attract me.

She wrote:
I'm unpeeling madonna, it's true, I'm opening up.

Writing as objective.

Fallen back we found ourselves with no pleasing
reply after so great an undertaking.
We gazed at our hands which bore no traces
on the lines and that's why we began to be
weightlessly different. Stretched over
the constructions, the cables permit
verifying that unsuspected junctions
are opening up/ the greatness/ and so the mixing
could extend forever, with unique
value, midway from that time
still without measure amidst all this
concavity. The buildings modified the
body and the gaze — with surprising
naïveté — hence the longing for light
from pits covered by another material.
A departure from the denial of life and still we didn't
know how to live it any other way because
inhabiting was the chimera: a way of hoping
terminally.

She wrote:
maybe they're not coming madonna, maybe tonight they're
not coming back.

Writing as illumination

In this city reconstituted/ out of some operetta/
the norm is effected only by restricting
imagery: then begins the spreading out of large
public panels privately dismountable
in continuous showings, enormous gray posters worked
in everyday names.
They are imagined:
in different poses, literaturesque and foreign,
antipodes of the foundation that still requires
religious decorations that hopelessly
adulterate it.
They wake up at dawn and me I pull up the
sheets pierced by something more unnameable
than terror.

She wrote:
they're humbug all these words.

Writing as mocking.

It was an illusion with fixed codes. Doped
from all the concrete it produced in us lucubrations
non-stop/ created notions of high
and low: the sun directing the mix.
They grew old from so much constructing. The fever
dropped to anachronistic forms/ empty and full
they demolished gazes. They did not leave proper
names. Rather they enjoyed in usufruct the
ones recorded on birth certificates. Anonymous styles
prevailed naming entire landscapes
in different areas, starting with drilled holes.
The era of those foundations was identical to the
machine era/ signs of noises:
feasts.

She wrote:
they imprison me, they bring me down those words.

Writing as abandon.

Forgetting that we have traveled this miserable
country with its name crossing its
chest in glitz letters, the name of
the same country that condemned us. Marginalized from
all production, delusively we separate ourselves
in order to indict the foundations. The sacred
was a gaming table in all its thickness — we didn't
bow down — on the contrary, we assumed now
in pure negation an amorphous and
agglutinative state that converts our minds
into foundations. And from all our protecting the head
the body ended up deteriorating.
By demolition, normed and transformed
we make our appearance in court.
You who didn't know me then never will know
a thing about my true thoughts.

She wrote:
they're fleeting words madonna, hardly even stammering.

Writing as erosion.

From tracing the streets that end up
opening other routes buried under the noises,
but insufficient for such brains who
appear prior to life's foundations,
excluded by birth. New foundations
like a trumpet call to Chileans
so they rest their backs on those machines that
elevate their brains by several centimeters.
It's been told to us that on these foundations there were
conquerors and conquered.
I say that's a half truth: there were
conquered and corpses. Nothing else.

She wrote:
it's true, the cables, the trees, the benches, the lawn, the
electric light.

She wrote:
illuminated entirely, turned on.

7

This isn't fair, I didn't see that scene.

— Don't hand me that line, said the man interrogating him. You were the only one nearby and that's why you broke her fall and then she spoke to you. Everybody knows that, just tell me what she said to you.

— It was something offhand, almost nothing. Really, it wasn't important at all, could've happened to anybody. It's hard to recall even, she was about to fall and I rushed over to support her. I don't know what she said. Maybe she thanked me. Everybody's had something like that happen to them. Anyway and that's just why I can't recall her exact words, most likely because they weren't of any interest: a thank you, some conventional politeness, answered the man.

— But you remember the scene then? Let's start anywhere. Describe what happened, the one who was interrogating said to him.

— I was walking past there, he answered, suddenly I saw her stumble and knew she'd fall if I didn't support her. I rushed over and grabbed hold of her, even though I only broke the fall, because her body sruck against the pavement anyway and I very nearly fell down myself. Afterward, I helped her up and went on my way.

— You stayed bent over her longer than usual. Why, asked the one who was interrogating him.

— Because I couldn't lift her, answered the man. I was in an awkward position myself, that's why both of us were struggling to keep our balance.

— The others came over? Anybody try to help you two? inquired the interrogator.

— Maybe, but I only managed to see the branch of the trees, the lighting cables. I didn't notice much else, really I didn't. From my position I saw only part of her face, then I lifted my gaze and caught a glimpse of all that. At that moment I couldn't visualize the others, answered the man. It was cold, he thought, it was dark. Actually that stuff about the tree branch was little more than a reflex, could be they weren't branches, or cables, or maybe it was the sides of her head that gave him that impression. From his position he managed to see almost nothing beyond the unobstructed view of her face which impelled him to images, but the other man had no way of verifying what he had seen. His statements were plausible. Whatever he said was probable.

He knew the tape was spinning somewhere. He had better be careful about what he said. Any contradiction was serious.

— But her eyes were full of tears, said the interrogator. You saw that, right?

— It's true, she was crying, replied the one they were interrogating.

— Why, asked the interrogator.

— It could have been pain from the fall, answered the interrogated.

— It could have been, said the interrogator, but it was not.

— And what was it then? responded the interrogated, seems like you're the one who has the answers.

— You made her cry. It was something you said to her, you took advantage of her fall.

— She didn't fall all the way, I held her up. I lessened the blow somewhat, emended the one they were interrogating, and whatever I said to her didn't go beyond comforting her. Clearly she wasn't crying over what I said to her. She could have been crying from before and maybe her clouded vision made her stumble and caused this incident.

The interrogator then looked at him and coming closer almost whispered to him:

— Don't be so sure of yourself. I have all the time in the world. Sooner or later you'll stumble too, hit a pitfall, and then in tears you'll tell me what it was you said to her, how you took advantage of her, how and why you ran across to support her and I'll be tired out myself and I'll have already lost patience with you. You're pretty satisfied with yourself. Think that might have affected her?

— Look, said the one they were interrogating, what you want to know I've already told you and it's not a matter of time. It's true she cried but I have no way of knowing why. And my attitude has nothing to do with that. You want something else. Why not come out with it once and for all.

— What you've got to do is answer my questions, just that, he warned him. Keep that in mind, and then tell me: how long had you been watching her? How was it you got to her fast enough to break her fall?

— I was walking by there, answered the interrogated one, and her appearance caught my attention, it was a matter of seconds. I admit I went a little out of my way so our paths would cross and I could get a look at her up close. That was precisely what let me make my move fast. That small detour motivated by simple curiosity. Anybody in my place would have done the same. Of that I'm sure.

— Did she look at you before? asked the one who was interrogating.

— Yes, she looked at me.

— Why do you think so, persisted the interrogator.

— Because our gazes crossed, answered the one interrogated.

— What did you think then?

— That I wanted to look at her up close, answered the man.

— So you went out of your way then, asked the interrogator.

— Yes, at that I moment I did.

— She tripped there and you came over and broke her fall, asserted the one who was interrogating him.

— That's how it was, he answered.

— But tell me: how could you see her eyes if it was dark?

— The streetlights illuminated the square. Besides there was a little natural light. Anyhow it was enough to see all that, said the interrogated.

— Or maybe you assumed she was looking at you or maybe she never looked at you because you were the only one who looked and the trees were protecting you and you were paying such close attention to her that when she passed nearby you came out of your hiding place in order to support her and then you told her something that scared her and made her cry. Maybe it was fear that made the tears stream down her face. It could have been that. At least that would be reasonable, said the one who was interrogating him.

— That's a preposterous story, responded the man. It was accidental, I already told you before.

— And then you thought the timing was right to approach her, the interrogator cut him off, because the innocence of the situation protected you. You were just somebody helping somebody else and that way what you told her was covered up because you had your mouth glued to her face and that's how you made your words almost imperceptible. And, although the two of you took longer than necessary to get to your feet, that was owing to the awkwardness of your position. Even those tears of hers could be explained by the surprise and the pain from the fall because her face, while she answered you, remained hidden by yours and the darkness in the square. It's possible, isn't that so? The interrogator had once more brought his face close to the man's and was speaking in a low voice, slowly.

— From one point of view it's probable. It strikes me as a good story, replied the man. But in the square that couldn't happen, I mean for somebody to be hidden by a tree and for her not to notice him beforehand. How could somebody have come into the square from any of its sides without having been seen? Walking under the lamps between the benches or cross between the bars of the fence in order to stay hidden in the grass? No, that wouldn't happen. It's all much simpler, I've already told you everything: our paths crossed under the light and that same light allowed me to see her and not let her strike the concrete.

He should not have spoken impatiently, not showed his irritation. Now the other one might get furious and lose his temper altogether.

That's why he added softly:

— I understand how you might think all that, especially if she cried, but the fact is that in the square what you say just couldn't have happened.

— You have lied from the start, said the one who was interrogating him, all that about the gazes and now that nobody could get into the square. It's too flimsy, all this stuff you're giving me. You're acting like an amateur. You know the difference between natural light and artificial electric light. Anybody can make mistakes. Camouflaging yourself is very easy.

— Under electric light? responded the man. No, that's not possible. The square isn't like other places. It's a circum-scribed space, regulated. Once you get to know it well you recognize anything odd right off. Nothing is innocent: the benches, the lawn, the lamps, the cables, they all have a particular, well-defined dimension. Any point of view is going to take in the others.

Daytime's something else, but at dusk or at night the movement is already programmed. The noise is pro-grammed, the people.

— For just that reason maybe, the interrogator interrupted him again, you knew exactly how to go about it so as not to be seen and you took advantage of the only break to get near her, touch her and speak to her, right there in the center so the whole thing would go unnoticed. But now then, let's finish: What did you say to her? It was starting all over again. It was like a circular scene rehearsed countless times. A scene gone astray, pointless. He thought about breaking this cycle, changing the point of view, switching to another subject that would unmask the weakness of its foundation. Start all over again but with another beginning. Modify his role, change the tone, undermine his exhaustion. But it was not possible, that's why he simply said:

— Nothing much, a few friendly words: that I was very sorry or something like that.

— How did she answer you, asked the interrogator.

— I don't know, I think she thanked me for the gesture.

— Where did the fall take place, continued the one doing the interrogating.

— In the square, in the middle of the square, replied the man.

— What made her trip, he asked.

— I'm not sure, maybe she stumbled from a bad step or perhaps it was a badly laid square of concrete or there was something on the ground she didn't see.

— What did you do then?

— I grabbed her fast as I could. Still her body struck the ground and I was on the point of falling too. I lost my balance because of the unexpectedness of the situation.

— Describe the position you two were left in, said the interrogator.

— She was on her side on the concrete with her head slightly raised. I had one arm resting on the ground and the other I put round her neck. Her head was practically underneath mine, but in spite of that the blow was softened.

— Could you see her face then, persisted the other one.

— Only part of it. Her profile really.

— What did she do then?

— One of her hands rested on the square's concrete and she raised the other to her head.

— Why did she do that, said the interrogator.

— Because she had something in her hand, something she pressed against her head.

— What was it?

— A piece of chalk, that's what.

— How did you see it, persisted the one who was interrogating.

— Because she was almost shaved bald and the chalk crumbled on her skull and fell to the ground. It even smudged part of her face and I felt it on my own hand.

— What did the others do then?

— I don't know, nobody came near us, answered the one they were interrogating.

— And why did she cry?

— I don't know, maybe she was crying before the fall, answered the man.

— Or maybe it was your words.

— I don't see why my words would have made her cry. It could have been the impact from the fall.

— And why did she have the chalk in her hand, inquired the one who was interrogating him.

— I don't know.

— But, persisted the interrogator, what do you suppose?

— That she picked it up somewhere, almost without realizing it and carried it in her hand almost automatically.

— It's impossible, the other one interrupted him again. That can't be true.

— I don't know, I don't have the slightest idea as to what she would be doing with a bit of chalk between her fingers.

— That act was premeditated, so that's why the chalk couldn't end up by accident in her hands; you know that perfectly well and I know it too. What I want you to tell me is what she was going to do with the piece of chalk.

The man looked at him and then said:

— Maybe she wanted to write something, people do that all the time, it's something childish. At least that's my impression.

— It's true, replied the interrogator, undoubtedly she was going to try that. But in the end, the fall prevented her. Because you've said the chalk crumbled on the ground, isn't that right?

— Of course, I saw it myself and I even had tiny particles of it on my hand. I realized that afterward.

And why do you think she crushed it against her head? Why do you think so?

— She could have been ill, she seemed confused because otherwise that action can't be explained. She seemed almost desperate or, at least, disturbed. Although after all it's not so strange; I've seen such things before. Some people are unpredictable, they have strange fixations on things.

— You mean the ones in the square: those are the ones who've got strange fixations — that's what you're saying, right?

— Yes, them, exactly.

— Why makes you think so?

— It's the fault of the setting: that monotony, the same solitude, the craziness of the lawn, the straying of the light overhead.

— And the benches?

— The benches strain your sight too. Their amorphous shape, the uncomfortableness and even the parallel cables end up irritating your eyes, making them red. All loss of will power is pushed to the point of blindness. The benches invite people to occupy them. Movement in the square produces order and makes sense of its organization. It's a set.

The interrogator and the one interrogated silent.

The carefully placed tape goes on spinning.

Possibly a film-maker frames them.

Someone transcribes the speeches.

— But it had rained in the square, asked the interrogator, you know that as well, right?

— Yes, but before, the previous day. It turned into dampness, the wooden benches, the grass, answered the one they were interrogating.

— And the cold?

— Sure, the cold, affirmed the one they were interrogating.

— You felt it?

— I was miserable, I was frozen stiff as a board, continued the one interrogated.

— And how did you manage to stand it, inquired the one who was interrogating.

— I walked fast, I moved around a lot, I crossed the square several times.

— Till you came face to face with her? asked the interrogator slowly.

— It was by chance.

— Chance?

— Let's start over again, said the one they were interrogating.

— Yes, replied the other man, that's the thing to do. Let's start over each time I want to. You should have understood it from the start. This always happens with beginners. It's a matter of patience, my patience. Go on, my friend: what did you tell her when you caught hold of her?

— I didn't say anything important, some conventional phrase.

— You were almost on top of her and her face was streaming with tears. I could say those words one by one but I want you to repeat them. I'd rather check the inflections of your voice, even copy your gestures. Do the scene over, reproduce that original. For just that reason tell me about the chalk again: how did she raise her hand to her head?

— You could never find out what was said, you're tempting me, it's easy to spot that, answered the one they were interrogating.

— But tell me about the chalk in her hand, insisted the interrogator.

— She crushed the chalk against her head, answered the one interrogated, smashed it at the moment when I broke her fall to stop her from striking the concrete.

— What did she write with the chalk? asked the one who was interrogating.

— I don't know, answered the other man.

— Or it could be you're the one who crushed the chalk against her head.

— That's crazy, responded the man.

— You did that, right? inquired the interrogator.

— What would I do something like that for? That's pointless. I'm getting tired of all this. What does it matter after all. What's it matter even if I did it myself. You want something else, you want me to tell you something else. Maybe everything would go much faster if you asked it once and for all.

— You think so? You really think it's unimportant? Look, nothing else interests me except verifying a few words, following a few gestures through to the end. By now the whole thing is over and done with. But answer me: why did you prevent the fall? It was scheduled. Why did you do it?

— I didn't want her to strike the ground. It would have been very painful. Maybe she'd have broken a bone, her head might have been injured. You know: the concrete, after all, anybody would have acted the same way.

— That's not true either. It was programmed, she'd readied herself for it. That's very serious: interrupting a scene, blotting out words, bending over her to talk to her, scaring her into changing expression. Making her lose her confidence. Tempting her, spurring her on to misgivings. That was your job. A slight shift of gaze, blaming it on the electric light. Are you satisfied?

— Yes, I did what I had to, it was my role, answered the one they were interrogating.

— That's true, but after the fall, without tears, without words, the gesture's what was asked of you, only that. But that's not how it was: you took advantage of the opportunity to make her confess, to detest, to take back what she'd said. You ruined the take.

— That's how it was.

— That's how it was, right?

— That's how, exactly how it was, but I insist that it was my role. It was bad writing after all. By rights the script shouldn't have included such a wallop. Not have her suffer a blow that way, after all's said and done, my action of catching hold of her was much more beautiful.

— She confessed, it's true, but she'd recognized the banality of her line. The forced reading. She cried, but not from pain, from the feebleness of her production. They couldn't swallow just anything. Not at all. Her body stretched out for nothing. Better to leave it like a rough draft. Like a rehearsal. That's what it was in short. Only that.

— But you went ahead and even out of the corner of my eye I could notice it. You were delighted with the fall. We were rolling and you didn't stop. You depended on reflectors, the light in the square wasn't enough. Camera in hand you were on the side opposite mine.

Really barricaded with your eye glued to the lens and your acolytes modified and synchronized the sound.

The interrogator rose and his eyes flared, he said:

— That my script was bad, that's what you mean?

— It was unsuitable rather, anachronistic, rough. Without technical effects only a univocal interpretation was possible. You confiscated the takes and in the darkness of the room I too was present for the projection of the rushes. I spied on your actions, your satisfaction, your eyes shining at the fall, waiting for the cut, the tinted curtain that did not fall. Your assistants were murmuring and there you were following the rhythm with half-open lips. You took the proof of the lines as real confirmation. You crushed the chalk between your hands and it crumbled until the lights came up.

The titles fell and the word was not formed, however.

He said:

— The girl lacked style, that métier announced by her presence was just something she borrows from her private life.

Those present agreed with lowered heads.

He said:

— And maybe that's why I took all this time changing the editing. I cut and took moments that were different from one another.

— You follow me? Stop that blinking, we'll have to tear up the originals. They're worthless, they're badly put together. Doing it over is a major undertaking. The girl, it seems she's retired or at least that she's doing something else now. We'll have to spur her into taking up her old tricks. She had other projects bigger in scope and livelier. But it's ruined, with so much light it wasn't any good either for iridescence or the stable word.

Manipulated she took upon herself the tragic tradition. But it was simpler, much simpler than that.

— I prevented the fall. I took her confession and the tapes support that.

They advance, they curvet, they wear out from so much replaying. They spin them at each sound and also their volume is raised on the board. The technician sweats, modifies notes, interrupts, adds sounds: distorts.

Through technology he produces errata.

At last those originals are redone. Her fall is imminent and the press awaits. The girl is properly posed. They announce the scene to the interrogator and to the one interrogated. They get their face ready, the witnesses wait. The under-pass is cleared to the point of being neutralized. The clothes are also right for the décor.

The man takes the camera. The interrogated one con-fesses. Her voice also appears, slow, utilitarian, thick.

It's true, says the man, I did see that scene:

I saw her stumble and I rushed over. That was the only moment to get near her and make her give up the staginess of the sequence.

I told her: if you fall now there'll be no possibility of redoing this stage. I told her: rub out the writing, it's no good, anyway you'll be criticized. I told her: get out of here, rest, think this over again. I told her: you're already considered one of the professionals, this fall is fragmentary, your speech is babbling. Redo the voice, correct the calligraphy.

It's true I elbowed aside the others who also rushed to see her, hear her strike the ground, make faces, try to steal a moment on camera. I blocked out these brazen tactics, I mugged my laughing at their tatters and I threw myself on her hard as I could. They recognized me at once.

He gave the word to cut, the machines stopped just when the girl changed her voice to say for the nth time "where you going?" which she didn't actually say, but safely in my ear she said "it's a waste of time they reduced me to frames and me myself to a letter and those others to actions, it's too much, I only had a few thoughts, a couple of meditations, plots almost."

But it's like this:
They run around looking for the originals. The files are full of diverse proclamations put in order for their final cataloguing. They pile up on the tables. Stacks of papers that already are part of the past. Somewhere else the machine keeps up the same pace: they ink it and the man gives the order.
The square is really almost empty. The cold has set in. Numbed she curls up on the bench. Smiles.
She has chalk between her fingers. The benches are in lines, the ground, the tree trunks, the lampposts.
It will be printed in typography, in offset, a gray stain will serve as a cover.
The light in the square will come up. The show will go on.

8

Dress Rehearsal

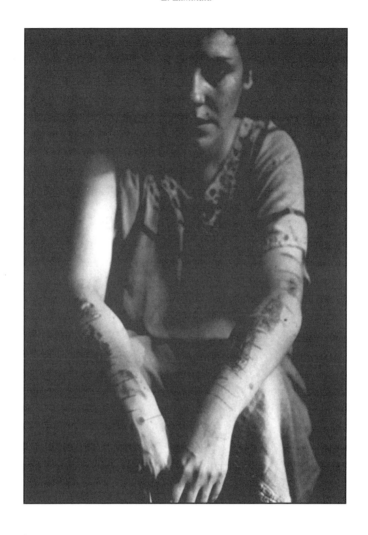

D.R. 1

She moo/s/hears and her hand feeds mind-fully the green dis-
entangles and maya she erects herself sha/m-an and vac/a-nal
her shape.

D.R. 2

She anal-izes the plot = thickens the skin: the hand catches =
fire and the phobia *d* is/members.

D.R. 3

She moo/s/urges round corp-oral Brahma her sig/n-ature ma
lady man ual betrays her and she bronca Brahamas.

Horizontal direction betrays the first line or cut on the left arm.

It is solely a mark, sign or writing that is going to separate the hand that frees itself by means of the preceding line. This is the cut by the hand.

Whereas — upward — the epidermis becomes bog/
                              barbered barbaric baroque

The second cut on the left arm is manifestly weaker. The blade has been sunk into the skin superficially. This second cut is ruled by the first on the left arm.

The distance that separates the two cuts is the surface of the skin that appears and emerges rigorously following the very shape of the wrist.

The third cut is flawed by interrupting in an oblique line the horizontal direction of the preceding lines.

It displays a wider swath of skin to the eye and the cut itself widens leaving obscured the birth or end of its trace.

The third line is discontinuous from the ones that precede it, despite preserving the straight direction.

The third line — gazed upon jointly with the others — betrays an erratum or rather the attempt to change course.

The first cut, if isolated, is the dress rehearsal.

Is it really a cut?
Yes, because it breaks with a given surface. On this same surface the cut sections off a fragment that marks a different limit. The cut should be seen as a limit. The cut is the limit.

Then, what is the border? The cut itself?
No, it's scarcely even the signal. The first cut establishes itself as dress rehearsal in so far as the others are successively integrated. In that sense its isolation is resorted to only so as to show the first mark that is established. The first cut is a seizure — it is a theft — on the plane of the skin's surface which is divided by breaking its continuity. A line is given so that it may be acted upon.

(Concerning the photographic cut.)

Is the cut represented in itself as in the photograph itself?
Rather it is fixed as such. The performance takes place to the
degree that the cut is acted upon.
For example, the track of the cut is a furrow that is operated
on by divulging it in that way as a signal. Yet, being like a
furrow, it becomes a trench or breastwork behind which is
protected or hidden a performance.
As furrow, it is sunk beneath a surface that has been penetrated. If it is restored photographically it becomes flattened
by the precision of a new surface, which will be broken only
by the eye that cuts its gaze there.

And what about the eye then?
The eye that reads it, erratic, constrained only by its own
contour, imprisons itself in a linear reading.
The eye that surveys the photograph stops at the cut (her cut)
and recasts the gaze when confronted by an annoying,
unforeseen interruption.

The cut's like that too?
Trompe l'oeil.

Let's suppose:

That the surface was chosen by chance and on it the first cut
was also made anywhere at all.
This way, the third cut could have been the first cut made. If
the obliqueness of its track is observed, it is perfectly possible
that that's how it was. On seeing that oblique result, it then
could have been corrected by instilling horizontality in all the
other lines. If that's how it was, then the first cut (which is the
third) did not end up freeing the hand, rather it marked a limit,
trace, border, trench, breastwork, between one part and
another of the arm.
Solitary, isolated this third cut — the first actually — is
scarcely graffiti on the skin of the arm that it enters upon
obliquely like a signature on a painting. Because it's curious
that this third cut should be the only one that changes its
direction in relation to the strict horizontal course maintained
by the others.

Is that perhaps why this third cut was the first and was made
shakily?
That's not likely. The third cut — by the oblique straightness
of its track — betrays no trembling course.
If it was the first cut, this deviation is explained only by the
whole scene's change to the horizontal.

What exactly does this third cut mean?
If first, this third cut is really the dress rehearsal.

Between the first cut and the cut first (the third) there is —
aside from the skin — a 2nd cut.
There is a second cut.
There's a second between cut and cut?
The interruption of a second between cut and cut?
Was there additionally a second after the cut? Was there?

The fourth line, on the other hand, is shorter than the previous ones, but returns to the horizontal direction sketched by the first and second cut on the left arm.

The track of the fourth line is briefly interrupted by a fragment of skin, which allows the supposition that:

a) The line was made in more than one stage.

b) The blade that made the cut was raised slightly.

The fourth cut on the left arm repeats the first and second marks, eliminating that way the oblique track which the third cut could have imposed.

The fifth cut on her left arm betrays its inlay over a new surface.

The surface on which it appears is modified by a burn on the skin. So this fifth cut is inscribed over (or under) the burned epidermis, which has in all certainty become bog/ barbered, barbaric, baroque in its weave.

The fifth cut as soon as it enters in relation with another form of attack, establishes the duality of the mark:

a) Cut that horizontally fragments the verticality of the arm.

b) Verticality that also is suffered by the trace of the burned skin.

c) Cut and burned skin doubly darkened by the darkness of the photograph.

The fifth cut, plus the burn is the rehearsal of the corporal scene.

From the previous scenes it follows that:

Defining the various cuts in isolation turns out to be subterfuge in so far as they are articulated to the degree that each
one is illuminating the course of the others.

(The efficacy of this broken surface is repeated gestural
research.)

It's plausible to determine an objective staging on the basis of
the marks on the skin:
Razed by the burn the down on her left arm disappears, the
raised scab, bristled over the burned down is another set for
the dress rehearsal.

The truth about the first five cuts plus the burns lies in
thinking of them, say, as pose and pretexts.

About the previous fragments plus the sixth cut.

1. Archaic sounds are mixed in with their art: recognizable quotations. Also registers from an old track also on their archetypal plane: the blade on which is written the brand.

2. The utility of their fragmentary element: the metallic and fine set of instruments recedes from the photographic trace. Everyday material. From trivial objects a pose is fabricated.

It has gone through. Her sixth cut is the apathy of the others, the vertigo and the habit.
The surfeit of the sixth element is a loose thread of burns, obsessive and fleeting it is scarcely marked along their edges. The in-cine-ration absorbs it and determines everything. It is appropriated from the linear space pushing, expelling the sixth cut.
Brutal seizure at the slash, but the skin blisters obscuring the sixth line.
The sixth line by its weakness is the rehearsal's surplus.

It's cold and maybe that alone is why she holds her pose in the square.

She sits down on the ground barefoot, her head bent slightly downward, she remains that way for a lapse of time and then raises her head and looks.

She keeps her sight fixed with quick blinks. The fingers of her right hand hold up the small sharp blade. Without looking she brings it toward her hide.

The Dress Rehearsal is going to begin.

9

Multiple Scenes
of Falls

LAST SCENES OF FALLS:

Sc. 1

Transformed into mere presentation she reorders her gesticu-
lating strap and formally unrolls herself revealing her own
malady. This time the track remains unblemished by errors,
she steps back toward the equal of herself and her old turns
start reappearing: rupestrian illustrious voracious

that they lead her to all this celebration. She falls so as to rise
again in this examinee who sticks to her own dubbing.
She curses/
        slapdash chromas her deception
    . a.w.a. sweating largo +
her name she doesn't manage to hook up with the light from
the streetlamp. Not that condition she had willfully established
on the inspected concrete. It reaches her
— the secular spot and tints her —
but not totally defeated she reviews the same available aliases
that had conditioned her. Hybrid and triumphant she's all set to
emerge: it's a question of light and this obstinate angle that
designates her there (but she always rotates so as not to let
herself become prisoner of the pose). Nothing subjects her to
immobility. Light and angle, they drive her aberrant, gesturally
wilted. She synthesizes the timid pencils of light that economi-
cally suture her/
she doesn't hesitate
in negotiating her particular limits. She plans her own manipulation in order to achieve her nearest equivalence. She is at the
edge of excesses and with the take of her gestures the preparation travels the whole broad space
of salvos like
        clarions/ inadmissible instruments/ the cold
        the
        seditious redubbed
everything that pours through the conventional orifices.
She heads out all over the lot/ doesn't succeed, however, in
establishing her own distance and is enthralled despite herself
in the shining mark.
She crosses her arms recompensed and evades the naming she

was about to reveal. She does not let herself be overcome by
the convenience of printing her extras, nothing calls on her to
stop at the shape she could establish. She cracks once more
what was receiving its final touches and her hand fingers and
crushes the fold, breaking this hypothetical binding

the thrust of the guillotine

that slices the leaf

cuts the vein and the trunk is scumbled as far as total curvetting.
Although harder the metal compels her to master herself.
So that it falls by means of lighting effects. More than boastful
she is contrite in her acuteness. Nothing demolishes her so
much as her own mannerisms which by enveloping her have
confirmed her particular style.
She confines them to her itch: topples them.

invades them

directs the scene and the scripts are divulged. Counterfeited by
images she renounces the stratified reel that demands one kind
of direction.
Melango tropo and cracking deafens
but, nonetheless, muteness only underscores her dramatics.
She ridicules the mistakes that a lack of material means might
commit her to.
She traces herself but in synthesis does not succeed in parcel-
ing out these insolences
she bleeds — perhaps — but neither reddens nor drips

nor groans

Sc. 2

She analyzes instead this way of prevailing and patiently
assembles her possibilities for adhering to a single alias.
Aroused by her chance luck she lets her hands wander to the
remainder of her scarcely mentioned zones — stretches them
— and her gestures then become professionally expert. That's
how it is, palm and skin are pleased and the branches of the
trees are turned.
She poses for no one/   neither is she
                              stretched out on the lawn so
                              precisely as the span of her palm:

palm and skin draw apart
not a hairsbreadth.

Sc. 3

Her tracks spread and there she fixes her crime. She's right
there and tranquility is not space gridded green, rather she
pants & the flush does not spread/ Nothing augurs: now
nothing is cold or frightens.
Marking off improves her preparation for attack. She locks up
the print run. Entangles herself in observation. Feigns.

     posing terrors she does not consent to, she tears
     by butchering her own arousal +
     responds
     with the tonality her marking requires.

Affronted she reaches her concreted space and moon down
speculates. She does not give way at all — rather — her hand
traces and she notices that skin stuck to palm her wisdom is at
the most primal
        of its roused heat

     She has embargoed the customary finery letting flow
     the lines that don't refuse to pass through veiled
     suggestion + gets hooked and the avatar atop her own
     darkness does not yield. Hunched over she captures
     this last singular alias.
     Guides it and raises it up — but — what haven't they
     aroused in her?
so as to roar once in a while she convulses from so much
membering herself drunk on this sole possibility/ she has said
     (twisted by final words)
"that there's no scaffold to support her." She signs apatheti-
cally and not caring has said, and the ordering of each one of
those letters displaces her feeble compliances.
She neither twists nor communicates this power that domi-
nates her on rare occasions when light surrenders to her lair:
                    digs herself in.
She opens for herself and splits from all the combinatorial that
designs her/ friezes and residues: not even.
She orders-unites-traces-elaborates-stays strict in her effect,
consistent in metabolizing her power because she disturbs and
grinds down her own ease.
But out of transitive stage she's in the
last throes, in order to retake her own turn &

does not achieve audacity.
She is not for this time and even less for this precariousness
that is being generalized.
They announce (proclaim)
                              the form of beauty but up she rises
                              knocking down her own buildings
Burlesque trap, hallucinated void that opens up gulping down
the light that emanates toward the reviled quadrant
Since they like it better if all lumpen
                                             shine.

Sc. 4

She decks herself out.
She decks herself out under attack to the point of refloating the
last spaces they've taken from them
she exhibits herself, muddles herself with them to contaminate
the outlawed.
She tells herself so many things, getting rid of the sparkles
from their salivating presences.
They slobber her with their tongue: they scratch out and mark
her speeches
      they bind her with fillets

      they remain excluded
if they risk their designation/ and / although they may get
upset often, the rough drafts are there stretching out like
swipes of a paw.
They wound themselves/   their defect is the razed head that
      has fallen behind like some incomplete get-up. They
      copy her stealthily and dolefully
      they all of them try to vent their fury
They use all her writing
her letters are already printed/   they misunderstand.

Sc. 5

Like rage the lumpenpack reveals itself. There are no
sillinesses for her to hide behind. Stiffened already from all
the handling her lip moans & twisted connects.
Emptied totally she rails against all the sordidness that from
her pritheeing skin/ she rummages around and gets there but,
nevertheless, the lights were suspiciously faint.
She repeats herself
she repeats herself and the experience conquers her own piling
it on/
her skin it yields
       cracks it does her skin and the blade delays the cut
Beautified she notices that the smoothness is still more
alarming. Skin and hide opened delicately are made ready +
she celebrates herself in her new condition and her legs resist
too but their solidity is only
          a matter of appearances
Of appearances whose direction can be followed. In its
luminosity the electric light casts shadows in switching.
She attends to herself
the hide hunches and she doesn't let herself be attracted by the
clinical impulse because she's afraid of so much weightless-
ness
    & speaks
but not one word matches her gestures.
She is mixed with electronic sounds, stepped up in suggestive
emotionality that cheers the gallery. It frolics with its own
elements and in its conventions
          the scene looks lighted:
the mark organizes, conceals, catalogues & her hide
nosed around
dazzles her.

Sc. 6

A census is taken of the material.
Hide and square dialogue when the latter's at her most
devalued. Its unkempt appearance disappoints the person who
crosses it, but they'll accuse that person of primitive steps.
The light falls and groping makes it passable.
More certain they cross it again to be touched again. With
light, hide and square's characters are blotted out and the lawn
barely hides the scab of ground that muddies it/

> hide & benches on the ground of the
> lawn.

Whimsies in their design break the precise fall so that forced
posing is the only comfortableness possible, but when placed
under the lamps
> under the square's light
they amass within all the deterioration condensed on them.
Nevertheless, some benches being hidden under the branches
break the sacred circuit of the night's darkness and deliberately blot out the stars.

> By bedazzlement/ of light and branches
> the benches are like the hide the wrinkled.

Sc. 7

Skin of light, courtyard, certain snare.
What a strange disposition this one's. She lies down in the
square and mortgages the license it yields her bet. She
bargains for success in provisioning her shocking splendor in
gray weaves that envelop her. She stigmatizes herself to the
point of extending her sentence:

She peddles it,
but without merchants' wagging arms
like skin and hide on sale that's all.
She doesn't push her confidence/ nor does she assault/ because
gamboling is the prosaic wrap that's achieved. She roars rather
at the stroke.
Bristles up maybe,
but doesn't return to the constant error, made live bait for light
she rears up another dance
cracks, yields, mocks.

She displays them and they've orificed the others, absurd
fleece so thick maybe, the notches can't be toted up: she rubs
their nose in it, dissolves them, errs and turns her face enunci-
ated by grooves
burned hide — yellowish furrows
they rise up and although the plane is being extended & the
skin rubs its touch up;
they have already given it back to her again so she would go
on imagining her omnipotence. Her hide, it got laid on their
foreheads. The light covers and uncovers the menacing path,
they engulf and lengthen it now that the square's at its best.
Now she has celebrated them all
& they're rolling to get back.

That's how it should have been and not even in their imagination were they able to do it, they hesitate so as to savor the
gulping down. Wood rasped on her hams — they cross her
splintering it — so why this tumble and her weaves being
spread: they rub out, pierce her shackles
They laugh.
They lengthen and the edges are clamping her orifices. The

flesh shines and sets off like a shot. She's put such distance,
has pierced them with shadow and surplus. Clean, she leaves
her razed head spotless as a sign. She sits down on the bench
and the backrest
                    trots her
                    jading her.
She grows feverish from all the squeezes she gives herself.
She glimpses the ray that irradiates her and settles into the
flintiest pose of her performance. She hugs, hugs the turn of
her railing and it's the lawn, the grass, the rain
                        that have stamped bites out of her outlines.
            She no longer even deciphers herself,
            rather she ruminates herself in the marginality of the
chink and is no more dynamic than all the crude imitation
dregs left over from all this wreckage
                        —thatched ruka or bog the square;
                        but not that either.
Hardened mixture, concrete, amalgam in her pores which
contract and expand in the manner of. Now she can't any
more, make her do the trick shot that perforates her. She
renounces the pose that in time past extended her magnificent
and on sheer impulse she reappears. The ground marks her.
Humiliates her. But still she covers her stigmata, takes up her
massages again and spread out the gray rags proliferate the
web & they shudder.

They touch and she's at the point of going back to her compo-
sure in the face of the whole illustrious droning
                                            The take falls
and they don't do justice to their decoration: they buck,
partialize, bellow.

            Now they've done it once again.

Sc. 8

She's really coming across, that square
she's about to make herself seen, yoked to her she rears up
once more.
She's firmer overall, firmer still/ excessive
But she once again gives herself to her, cedes herself to her in
order to later recover their inquisitive gaze. She allows her
apex to be invaded, readies it for craving/ renews it salival
                        and the moan explodes
Explodes and it is crystalline substance that emanates.
Like a bubble her moan bursts and consumes in water but it's
her hand that appears to be consumed in the fire.
She likes that and always has liked it when she brings out the
shine in the hide that hunches her. She rubbed it against
herself: Lady Muddy she might have been called but she
didn't catch the signal. Nothing's as planned and they formulate nothing.
The square roars — really they'd like to start jawing.
Her hand in the fire
of appearance wears thin and it is the easiest crystallization of
the scene.
From special effect to special effect
comes misrepresentation until compelled she half closes her
eyes so that her gaze hides her from the conventional take.
But not to put on even more of an act, she is consumed by
prissy instinct leaving her perforation covered.
                      She was already burning at that hour
It was already hurting her, for sure, but her
               baroquetry — her boggedangling turns around.
She lied: she cheated at the last minute and that was her
pretext for ascending into the void dismantling the fleeting
expectations.
She doesn't really lacerate, doesn't manage to disassemble it.
She lied and she cheated with her hand in the flame
                           but she likes that.

Sc. 9

Fans have come out to gratify their eyeballs. The waste from
the drunken spree has already been submitted to this event.
They are paradoxical in their excesses. They don't lay it on
thick any more, they don't convince. But as for that woman,
she flames up with truth and beauty.

Articulated in the fault she curbs herself.

She welds her wasteland jitters, joins them with difficulty but
gets nowhere: she will not consent to magnifying her whole
passage with rejection.

She lets herself stay in the square until light illuminates the
whole lumpenpack and since they name her, she has resorted
to the vast subterfuge of cheating in order to cancel them out.
Without denominating it has been said or at least
the provisionality that without naming itself names them and
alters them.

She has hawked ankylosis on her posters and announcements,
on the square's banners stretched out like her craziest phrases,
banner phrases she's said and that way she doubles the letter's
authority/

They reject, they deny, they sermonize her
They try to dignify their harangues, they pester her with
preparations.
They tremble her.

She lied, was at the point of erring, they leave her bovine from
prescriptions,
but they could not control the fascinating escapade:
the brilliant streetlamp where by bedazzlment she lay before
them her apparent privations.
Interrogated down to the sediment of nonconformity
                                                    she pleyntes

But again they copy her so as not to get left behind. One by
one she starts up with the quit bugging her like that/ she hides
behind an apparent lassitude: deceives them again.

They believe her every time because they're scarcely trading
cards, flimsy superficial scaffolds, glorious in their finitude +
lumperrant they ought to know: to touch them, we're just
going to rub them a little.
But it won't be like that: they display literaturesque modes, in
their tasks pedantic, in type antiquated.
Racked by another dreadful light they look for her as far as the
bench; she dwells in them and calmness hands her over. She
pulls out her best bits
and catalogues them in her labors/

> she seeks them delicately
> la tan sua
> in order to charm them

     — it's part of her job —
now she triumphs from this angle upon marking them with
serenity, leaving them in the mastered middle distance. She
then contested once again her proper name and resorted to her
most flamboyant aliases/

> lumperrants got caught up in her drama
and she was able to squeeze out of them what also lacking she
sought.
They were made: day after day the lucubration was increasing.
Without news of any sort, the square was then the show place
for an apparent civility.

They win her for the experiment to the point of rubbing out
every other kind of inscription. That way she is tamed by joy
and concedes.
Concedes and breaks with her unpublished proposal.
She slipped in via light on the benches, she pulled out her
successes via cables
— violated the matrix —
Incrusted with fame she fell to the grass.

Sc. 10

Razed head down her atrophy has crumbled. She has been put
on track in a business complete with the apparition of these
pariahs who still break their arbitrariness
>   error and shine their looks
>   + she hawks her wares
and on uninterrupted schedule she traffics in them with all the
volubility with which she accepts this tinselly merchandise.
She has left them like mere graffiti in the square.
The error mounts and produces in her the semblance of
happiness. If it went even further, if errata covered everything,
if the fault alone cracked her indelible success, if she tri-
umphed by sheer juggling, if she spurred the popular expectation, if she changed roles by always descending.

>   they mock her use her unsettle her

She rises and by camouflage has been elevated and she makes
a strike against the night
the track
>   the track lacerates stretched across the square
>   & wounded by her
>   she pleyntes
her predisposition to ascent/
creaks that way but does not give up.
Does not give up but is softened by a kind of pallor that
pierces and her hollow loses effectiveness.
>   why's she scratching her hides?
She is ploughed by obstinacy and the parted skin places the
intrusion/
>   the true rush is consolidated in perpetual
>   aggression and that's how they pass over her by not
looking at her;

>   She rises again in a final out-take

It is said/
She bleeds.

Sc. 11

She bleeds scant emanation and although it does not spread: it
tints, with luxurious expenditure her out-of-sync presumption.
What do they think?
about this reassembled square that does not produce the de
luxe sepia side: she crosses because her tones do not contrast
sufficiently and that's why she moans, being faded into
bottomed-out coloring. Perhaps branches inculcated their rosy
blushes in her or better yet to botanical turnings an appeal was
made at her height of heat.
Branches surely brought her the troubled effect in the conjunc-
tion with the lawn, benches welcomed her, cables tensed her

& lights

— she the lumpenluminated —

The lumpen crack their booming pose and clash, discharging
better their manifest complacency/ they see her/ they divine
her and let her pass in order to conceal the open hide.
They push her with pure light, but she extends herself so as to
ennimble them, so that they may order their statements, she
treats them:
the chalk manipulates a big white splotch/

hooks them.

She possesses them in high-flown furrows that the letter digs
out as though the lawn were ruled off in filigree beneath her
quakings: they spoil it as pavement/ she attempts to hawk:
preaches grotesquely and they cast lots for her in her lapidary
infula/
they restore her to her low style +
humiliate her but now the blush spreads and the grass/
the springy grass, crushed down beneath their bodies

does not bristle erect.

Nor even cut
she raises her head when they approach collecting their trash
and driving out the storytellers who glitter tinseled light.
Cut with the blade of sharpened backstitching:

she hallucinates.

Sc. 12

Castillian spirit she's displayed in order to resituate her
designed space: healing she's obtained in scars/ tracks whose
constancy blunt the diminished surroundings.
They plunder her every referent
more than the square's light, she awaits lumperratic judgment/
     completely inexpressible
in her toppled continental pedigree.
     They demolish her
with such inventiveness, that it troubles only the initiated
              So
that's how she constitutes their human material: with surplus
pariahs she has recovered by electrical lighting effects in the
square & as if by a trick

    saves the darkest hour, of wakeful light
    insomnia yields its fleeting drive + opens the wound,
    she reformulates the gesture, peels off the scab/

      licks her stitches.

Sc. 13

Technical devices always upset her. Cables, perhaps, and she
dreams of being transformed into a parallel track of the absurd
hook-up: she blots out visions, settles her stay, sets up bargains
in damaged pyloruses already abjured of her ancestral counte-
nance/
        She grows
and it is the hour when her face is deformed — she nods —
but does not fall again rather she changes benches
                — wood for stone —
                          and seats
herself on its platform. She moves her leg, bristles her
feelings, energizes the shape of her rubbed aspect & turns her
sight on the ragged people/
                moves her hand + those people they resist.
She pays homage to them, praises them, aiming at supplication
for their admiring gazes: they're satisfied.
She snakes across the square. From ordinary margin she
moves the gesture of the burn away from the concrete. She has
turned her particular order inside out hindering any certainty/
                              she really
doubts regrets the sign, all information is distressing and all
the documents
            are temporary
In cold setting, in frozen aspect numbed she groans to cover
herself, it will dawn — surely — it's getting near a generalized stone cold of the homeless with no roof over their head.
                            They curl up
only posing. They turn
to the fire and kindle its remains, they camp by the light that
reflects them, they serve meanwhile her cold image, the
compassionate one's human complicity.
A circuit is opened, the set-up specified, recapped in synthesis:
they seek her out in order to defeat the cold;
            she submits so as to be gracious to them.
They search her in fact in order to squeeze her tightly and she
sees only beams from the illuminated sign, beyond and
discharged of mythical anachronisms.
                  Technology imposes
wildly snarled
disturbances:

witchcraft is installed in the electric light's hook-up/.
neonic indecency, howls manufactured in synthesizers,
splutterings. Names are cast in order to be reformed + aliases
are oversupplied in this dealing out of all the loose ends of
identities so that it's no longer known what civic act degraded
them by naming them.

Sc. 14

Maybe that's how they transgressed their useless ragged look,
they avoid touching them and that way they lose the luxury of
their flesh.

They brawl all out upon setting aside their good behavior, they
penetrate like an imposed totality, they delve concentrated into
their hindrances. They suppurate at the same time their
imperfections.

> They observe her, those toothless ones they smile,
> she leaves them fixed in their gazes. She has reviled
> herself.

Scraps of lumpenesque order unravel the striated exploit/ she
atomizes by taking them out of their referents

> — that the wound permutates through her scars —

> she ages she toils and she doesn't levitate.

She grants nevertheless for balance that things be established
in inscrutable style/ she hates her distant vertigo that was
casting her spirit downhill/ from simple distraction she dyed
her anatomy with rage and audacity dragged her toward the
gesture: she wavered — maybe — in dazed effort to contain
the remainder she still held on to,

> she suspends it, postpones it in vain:
> will the day of the attack come?

Yes
and she will stretch out in the square without her rough drafts,
will let the lawn infect her. For the sake of seeing once more
the frieze of her legs she will graze the benches, look at the
cables, be caught by electric light: straightforward and
suspended, fever of memory. Her distant story no longer
works.
It's all behind her now,
been tough this run-through of the sponsor she has given
herself for returning at this point, undecorated,

> detached image of decorum.

She does not grow/
does not radiate, they do not enjoy her, she does not inspire.
In fact she wears herself down in the trivial turn, hides her

face and her gaze. All she's got left is this lumperrata which on
the outside is scornful of her/
                    they postpone her until this dawn &
                    she bleeds.
She bleeds in order to take back her territory, scarcely the
gleam in their gazes.
She opens, clips, acknowledges when all splendor was
delivered to her by luminous feeling/ when from the atmosphere of light she rose, bush and frieze, rubbing and grass,
noise rather was heard from her.
                    Her skin splits icily, her blood
is scarcely a chink, convention deceives + joy on the other
hand mounts: the surprise of the spelling obviously dissolved
into rhetorical trills
                before that cleared space.
Here we go again,
and once more that livid hide is opened, stabbing risk of the
fevered surroundings: she lies down,
lies down really so they will lick her and it's her own mouth
that takes pleasure, she licks for herself their emanations,
bypasses iconography, jumps again to technology and crosses
sounds, recomposes her mood, awaits on the ground her pose
                    & transgresses.
Licking, licks, laps up she gives herself the imaginary name
for life.

So much nonsense for her padding: blanks, beats being
distorted so that now maybe never can she return to her
eradicated center. It's not exactly signaling a deal/ it's not that.
It's that they have set her before her own eyes.
It's that they give her the bum's rush and the square,
        only the square sees a difference in the gesture.

Sc. 15

Jaded she pants with lust lazulied + eases up the frost on
thirradiated plain amain with the forces of nature and
insufflates resonates resuscitates bogs the calm and illustrious
draws to its tautest the epicurean border of lassitude and
terrible deceit they infect her & she annunciates her scattered
matrix clot of commonplaces threadbare announces and
nuances with gilt gold the sun-drenched ambiguity usually
containing evocations + into hymen pours lumen and maybe
the lighthouse of iridescence buzzes its splendor resonates the
weak mark and sweating her opulent shimmying backside
from all the effort couples but the pack leaves her behind in
the stampede she lets go with her auraed curvetting and the
flame of the burned forest ruts ruddy like her burning bush
silent the snaking path dribbles + the ground is cracking her &
bosses her around she quivers and from a pennant pendant she
quivers at her full height + crying it spreads her as far as
crumpling her and its pecking frightens + she sweats at the
mouth + that happens to her + she moans + who is it imprisons
her in this falsettoed that's on offered lumperratic and who is it
constricts the anus that's whipped in the phosphorescence
more altered in her doom instead opens her haunches in
pustules of fear + the conquest breaks the mounting and blazes
open her moist latency out flow sumptuous fantasies she shuts
her palm the trinket she licks that seethes corrupt clumsy
oakum and she doesn't throb that fibber being turned into
glaring back grimaces & the square splits the ear drums now
she'll not return to the starting side + the hymened branch
grazes her on la sua figlia and on comes tharboric the
concupiscence & it's the wood that arrives the nodding off
madonna who nods her spellbinding of leaves and branches so
servile so weepy with nostalgia that she undresses that haunch
in innocent folds and penetrates on the tamed lawn without the
Lares thimmortality is summed and it's ceded and it's agape
thentrance to the sepulcher the lair hymenic is laric + now she
neither pulses as in time past nor embraces the ragged woman
& her vein bows to the lumpenpack when inche I myself
crossed gazes in fanfaring sufficiency & from the nasty place
she traces & roars all her names of unnamed alias surnames
like an extension of grass on their flat plain that beguiles some
& it's from nausea & vertigo that she cries most the gruff

parquet will arrive late devouring her in heat and the
lumpenpack all round with salvos and shots will explode up to
the barred gate and will becry the whole thigh + they serve her
prodigally & attack her with such accustomed shamelessness
by means of star-seeing blows that over them the night sees
light of day and her vein may be seen this farsical figure may
it be seen like that + she laughs and she sweats in vomits or
deaf explosions that show her her unaccustomed laugh + she
makes good use of them roughhouses still and the trees shine
as though they project from her + she yes crouches
and trembles maybe weakens her remarkable appearance? she
falls back on the old trick of studied gesture but goes back to
posing disillusions herself that one there & they're her legs the
woods' projecting branches and she rears up the wine vine's
must that warbles dribbles + lake and shape in her luminated
the blaze that spreads over all the razed & dry & smooth-
cheeked welkined wenumapu the quena the cut a trail her
figure and it's seminal the slime on her hand in the foliage
when she concealed her face and her face then was the mark
of her fingers dancing her the whole phantasmagoria that
twitched her mouth into gape + grabs ahold she does of the
chisel and opens her hide she bleeds again at herself looks and
her blood doesn't know where the stain's from all the light that
rears red on her + absolutely lovely she now is at daybreak in
the public square + what kind of chalk was that to hold on to
it? what parts did it mark? what filth? bogser down +
luminates her eyes looking forward she welds prithee opens
her legs & says I'm thirsty from constant huffing she says and
threshes and dupes the irony + l'ame uneasy her matrinal pose
she renounces per piacere perhaps when struck quaque tu she
had to say to the lawn and dumped her sky into the trash can
and followed the ceremony with eyes closed and she takes
account of the trunk that spanks with branches and rubs it and
her péctore and it's she who throws on the bench her miserable
mane and it is firelight.

10

She is alone in the square. Seated on a wooden bench with her head leaning against its back. A few people still linger there and nightfall gives notice that the lights will soon come on. She looks at them absent-mindedly. She is holding a paper bag on her lap.

She is wearing a gray dress rather longer than what is in fashion. An almost shapeless dress cinched at the waist by a cord, also gray. She does not manage to strike a brilliant figure, though certainly one somewhat jaded or scarcely noticeable. The dress that covers her is made from heavy fabric to ward off the cold that has fallen upon Santiago. Her gaze manages to distinguish the cars going around the place. They drive with their headlights on and they light up the square. It is a busy time and that's why many people cross diagonally through the square, taking a short cut. They are all more or less bundled up. The couples chat while walking, but no one is just strolling along, rather they are headed some-where else. She has a panoramic view of one limited section, enabling her even to make out fairly clearly those passing by on the opposite sidewalk, presenting the constant of their striding along with a certain haste, as though the weather pushed them into hurrying their steps so as not to get too cold.

The vendors, who up until now had been hawking their wares, are also taking down their rickety stands, getting ready to leave. No one makes a move to buy anything. The vendors are packing up their bundles and carrying them off without apparent effort.

Gradually, those who remain seated on some few of the benches start rising to their feet. People of different ages move about and cross the square. They leave various things on the benches such as papers, newspapers, wrappings, small plastic bags, and similar objects. But they do not manage to make the square look dirty, even though some of these things remain lying on the ground.

She stays there and now her eyes are keeping track of the people leaving the square, trying to distinguish them from those passing through to save a few steps or who have cut across it merely by chance.

The branches of the trees rustle in the wind. The lawn is plainly neglected and bald patches of dirt show through. The railings protecting it are also rundown and their green paint discolored and chipped.

All this is visible to her in the angle that her eyes manage to encompass. She remains seated with her legs crossed in front of her and her feet resting on the ground. Her hands press the paper bag firmly onto her skirt, but without squeezing it very hard. From time to time she crosses and uncrosses her legs slowly while her head turns to watch the pedestrians walking near her or is attracted by the sudden braking of some car that can be seen blocked in traffic by another.

The square is now almost empty and enclosed by darkness. She scarcely manages to make out a handful of people seated on the benches, not being able to distinguish them in any greater detail, since the visibility renders them only in silhouette.

The number of pedestrians on the sidewalk opposite also decreases. They are no longer seen walking in clumps, but with spaces between them, most of those passing by being men. Their clothing standardizes them and that effect is compounded by their even height which makes them repetitious and monotonous, especially in the poor light that prevents any feature from being singled out.

Suddenly the lights are turned on, just when it was almost totally dark.

They come up slowly, first casting the area in a dirty tinge which gradually grows more intense and sharper. The light in the square follows the same process as the streetlamps placed over the surrounding sidewalk. The perspective changes with the lights turned on, since what is under their bulbs shows in false yet clear shades, whereas the rest, which is farther away, remains backlit.

She is quite near a streetlamp and that's why she becomes visible to any observer. Her position has changed slightly. Now she is sitting on the bench a little hunched over, but her legs are no longer crossed, while her feet still rest on the ground. Similarly, she no longer has the paper bag imprisoned in her hands, instead it has fallen all the way onto her skirt.

Absolutely no one else is left in the square. The benches are empty and movement is noticeable only along its fringes. Cars keep going by, as do pedestrians who walk the nearby streets in ever fewer numbers, usually alone or in much smaller groups. There are stretches of time between them and that's why their footsteps resound, making it impossible for them to walk by unnoticed. This way from the square the street appears like a set and in the same way the pedestrians, actors crossing it. It is a ghostly set in its desolation, its emptiness, but right now it occupies all her attention. Each person who walks by in front of her is intently observed by the woman who follows them until the individual passes out of sight. Occasionally her interest is interrupted by some car that causes her to lose the figure, then she manages only to catch a glimpse of the passing head. She studies their way of walking, the things they carry, the style of their clothing. And this way she can gauge how great is their hurry and how deeply the cold pierces them or not.

Although she can determine only superficial aspects of each one, because of the short lapse of time during which they appear before her eyes, she dissects them even so. She also watches, when nobody is walking by, the neighboring build-ings.

From her point of view the square is bounded by three streets, and that's how she manages to see parts of each one. The houses are low except for a building silhouetted on one corner. The colors at this time of day are not vivid but pale, giving the buildings a vague cast in their dimness.

For the most part, the houses are similar in style: a door and two, sometimes three windows onto the street. In some of these windows, light betrays the occupants' activity, light that allows a glimpse through the translucent shades over the windows. Once in a while she manages to make out the profile sketched by someone moving about inside.

The doors open directly onto the street and their dark color makes them stand out immediately. During this time, no one has gone into any of those houses. Perhaps they did before, when the crowd of people prevented her from noting the fact.

In contrast to the low height of the other constructions, the outline of the building stands out there like some different and even jarring place. It is neither very high nor very modern, its narrow windows do not appear to have any balconies. It stands exactly at the corner of one of the intersections. Some of its windows are lit up as well and others not, which would appear to be some odd game of chance and might even be played with the nearby sign flashing its reflections on or off across a gaze. But the turning on of lights in the building is haphazard, not giving rise to any hidden meaning.

There is a large gate between the entrance and the interior illuminated by too weak a light. Differing from the other constructions, this one's entrance reveals some steps leading up to the apartments. No one has gone into this building during this time either. The stillness is absolute especially because of the diminished number of cars. That's why the sounds come now from farther away, from some place that cannot be determined any more than as nearby, surely produced by vehicles circling through the neighboring streets.

One of the most distant houses in her angle of vision has a roll-down steel grate, which indicates the presence of a store or a workshop perhaps. Something impossible to read from this distance is written across its façade.

Her steady gaze enables her to discover that of the few cars going by almost all belong to the police patrolling the streets.

She no longer studies anything so steadily as before, rather her gaze moves back and forth across the familiar spaces without finding anything that entices her. The area's inertia is almost total, if it were not for some undeniable straggler still made visible by his obvious haste.

For example, the last one went by almost on the run. With his lapels turned up to ward off the cold.

She is now almost curved over on the bench herself and she often moves her feet to keep them from going numb. She no longer holds the bag on her skirt but has set it beside her on the bench. Her hands are crossed and from time to time she rubs them together. Once again her legs have crossed, resting on the ground. Sometimes her head stumbles so far forward that she might be overcome by sleep. But with the fall of her head she gives a start and then immediately erects it, opening her eyes. She shifts position briefly but soon returns to the former one in which she is comfortable.

Her eyes now follow the lines of the square that reveals itself in another dimension after being vacated. The lighting is not equally good all over and the height of the trees fills broad stretches with shadows. The lamps expose the cables that supply the light and are another point of reference for the boundaries of the square. The bulbs are not very bright, betraying their age. A couple of them are even burned out. But the square is visible, especially part of the lawn which, radiated by shadows, is cut by the specter of the tree.

The concrete squares are more sharply delineated than in the center of the square, which most of the benches face. Oddly, there is nothing in the center: no playground equipment for children, no fountains, absolutely nothing, as if its only decoration were the whitewash spread over the tree trunks which actually helps to make their design unsightly.

The concrete squares, in spite of their placement, produce a vast aridity and frigidity in the place. Gray is the dominant tone here, to which is added the color of her dress, denying any advantage even to the green on some benches that have lost their shine. Farther off among the trees are the stone benches, placed along narrow pathways that lead to the sides of the square. These benches are gray too, though of a lighter shade than the rest.

She cannot succeed at taking in the whole square from where she sits. One portion lies in back of her and two others are also almost in back of her, but it may be presumed that what she has seen is repeated all over the place. It does not look like a site designed for recreation. The absence of color is one of the foremost problems, and also the neglect evident not only in the benches, but especially in the patchiness of the grass. Although it is true that by day the presence of people gives it a different look. Besides, many details would have escaped the notice of others.

Suddenly her eyes no longer proceed with their steady watching; they start wandering from one spot to another, as if reviewing her previous observation, hoping again to find a sign of something different.

Once more it seemed as though she were about to be overcome by sleep, her head began to fall upon her chest and the succession of sudden starts went on and on. At each one, she darted rapid glances around her as if someone might take her by surprise, or something, perhaps, might have changed. With one of her dozes, longer this time, the shudder afterward was also greater. Then she got up from her seat as if afraid of leaning against the backrest and really falling asleep.

She walked toward one side of the square and sat down on the stone bench nearest her path. Falling asleep was not possible that way: the hard, uncomfortable bench prevented it, unless she stretched out on it.

Seated this way, she accentuated the curvature of her back almost to the point of letting her chest fall onto her skirt. Her hands propped on her knees to support the weight of her torso, her feet splayed to strengthen the position.

The location did not change her perspective much, although perhaps this had more to do with the monotony of the area. Now the lights were out in the houses and the building. That's why she paid more attention to the sign placed high above.

The luminous sign's own light brought into view the framework of its scaffold, constructed from metal and wood so as to provide a better support for the heavy sign.

It went on and off at intervals. The predominant color of its legend was red filtered through neon tubes that calligraphically shaped each one of its letters, framed by other neons in various reddish tones.

It had two legends and so, when one blinked off, in the next lighting up it was the other that appeared.

She watched attentively, and she ascertained that the different readings resulted from the functioning, surely by means of synchronization, of separate sections in the signboard. Her eyes stayed riveted there and she fell under a kind of spell that prevented her from changing the direction of her gaze.

Not because she was waiting for something unusual to appear there as if by some act of magic. It was simply the attraction of the light.

Not even the pain in her eyes could distract her. She was completely dazzled. She practically could not read the phrases as they took shape and she even raised her torso in order to further elevate her gaze toward the top of the building. She remained absorbed; the various neon tubes crisscrossed in curved and straight lines, turned on in one part and then in another, revealing the apparatus that constructed them.

She had already seen it before, but it had not cast such a spell over her, surely because of the numbing sounds in the square, the aimless wandering of the people, her own lack of attention.

Now everything was different. The dizzying play of the sign was the perfect pattern for her gaze which, flooded with pleasure, had surrendered. Although she wanted to change her view she did not succeed, she waited for the change of legend and then the next until it became a vicious cycle.

Because the luminous sign would not stop.

It was programmed for the night and its program did not have the rationality of a Chile that halts its rhythm at night. That's why all alone as she was, subjugated, it was she who had received the message, not of the product but of the sign itself, of its existence as such. She thought she should stop because her eyes were saturated from the effort, but she delayed until the next time it lighted up and then the next and she could not

take her eyes away. Nothing else occupied her thoughts, until
an idea emerged from her brain: that whole show was for her.
She knew with certainty that no one else at this hour was
hanging on that sign's legend, so this lavishness was meant for
her. Someone had mounted this costly special effect in the city,
as a gift for her: with writing and colors, with colors and
motion, engineers' calculations, manual labor, permits. All this
so that she, seated in the square at night, might really let
herself be carried away by the blinding light from those glass
tubes which insufflated with colors, powered by batteries,
would subject her.

Even her weariness disappeared in the dazzling light. The
rigidity had vanished and this caused her to reappraise not
only the square but also the houses near the sign.

She thought she was not in harmony with the up-to-date
technology that pleased her so. Her clothing, her whole
appearance was almost a crime against that brightness and
activity.

Perhaps she could have taken greater satisfaction in herself if
her clothes had had a few modern touches, something singular
that also might have denoted her as unique in that strange
situation.

But that's not how it was.

She was there in all the modesty of her gray dress. Although
suddenly that seemed right to her. The antagonism between the
observer and the observed created an evident tension, whose
mediator was the advancing night in the public square.

That's the only reason why for the first time she could tear her
eyes away from the top of the building, in order to let them
fall upon the squaring of that space, and that way, she compounded falsification upon falsification.

In the midst of that artifice maybe she was not real either.

The uselessness of both — square and sign — in the night
struck her with full force. Even she herself was an excess.

She stood up and looked at her hands, her feet, her clothes.
But at her, who was looking at her?

When she was no longer herself, but what the space had
constructed from her continuance there, what the sign had
given her by putting ideas in her head with all the letters it had
cast upon her eyes, until the initially encoded had been
successfully decoded.

Letter by letter, word by word, during those hours when she
wore out her gaze letting her eyes wander over the neons,
avoiding the apparent messages that might have led her astray
if she had remained on the surface of the text.

But no.

She had succeeded in uniting the most far-apart letters, the
turned on and the switched off, the crisscrossing of the two,
the signs they constructed in between, the apparent blanks, the
interchange between message and message.

Everything was clear now and that's why she was able to
begin glancing from house to house with their lower portions
illuminated by the intermittencies of the sign.

Actually, it wasn't only the square's light that radiated beyond
its borders. The sign's light also tinted those lower stories, just
as other light affected, modified the sidewalk and the street
and even the trees, exactly like herself who perceived the fact
with absolute clarity.

And in truth that lighted advertisement had a defect: the height
of the building on which it stood. It was not sufficient and
that's why the neons were not being diluted as they ought to
have been but, like the sun's rays, painted their surroundings.

That's why she got up from the stone bench and for a few
moments had to move her hands and legs to bring them back
to life. Relaxing her neck she stayed rigid. She saw the sign
projecting itself onto her gray dress. Some red lines crossed
her dress. Not sharply but like light reflected from above. She
changed places, moving a short distance away from where

earlier she had been seated for so long, but always following the direction of the illuminated sign. It was the same. Some vague markings of colored light reflected on her, rose-hued at that distance.

She tried different ways of shifting from one place to another and in each one of them she was still imprinted by the sign.

This was most evident toward the middle of the square where she stood with her back to the major street that circled the square. Here was the precise angle at which the light from the sign fell most strongly, managing to denote some letters that, very diluted, never succeeded in forming words. But the writings open to more than one interpretation occurred there. Each one of them contained more than a single letter.

She pulled herself together against the cold in the center, where it was not diminished by the trees and she spread out her dress with her hands. That was it. Now she had the missing element. She realized that light at that moment was also falling across her face, her hands, her feet: across her flesh.

She tried to figure out which sign was falling on her, gazing for that purpose upward to where the luminous signboard was suspended. She remained absorbed in that a long time, calculating in the distance which letter most likely corre-sponded to her position. She wavered between a couple of them and also on account of the distortion of distance, which could change one into another.

She decided to give it up for a while until she became calm and entirely lucid.

She must not make a mistake and believe erroneously that she was imprinted with a letter that in the end had never really been hers.

She returned to her initial place, but this time her eyes were riveted on the center of the square. She saw there the falling of the letters, which although diffuse, were presupposed by the reading she made of the ones emanating from above. To do that she sat down again on the stone bench which provided her a better view. She made herself comfortable on the seat, but a sound distracted her: with the hem of her dress she had let the paper bag fall to the ground. She bent over to pick it up and she placed it on the bench again.

She realized after a quick look that it was impossible for her to specify an accurate combinatorial with certainty. Which two, three, or four letters might fall on her if she stayed in one definite spot. And even more than that: owing to that same distance, some letters piled on top of others, giving rise to complete words, which beyond any clear or precise meaning established links among themselves.

Besides, all this depended on her absolute rigidity, which was totally impossible because of the prevailing cold and each one of her movements would permit the appearance of other signs and that way of various words.

She stood up after a while and began pacing the center of the square. Her gaze wandered over the lawn or else rose above the top of the trees until it fell on the lamps. She did that for some time. The cold was intense. It was the moment when night wastes away as such, in order to yield shortly to the first glimpses of dawn. That's just why, maybe, it was a limit-moment at which the electric light most efficiently illuminated the square, which now stood out differently than at earlier hours, when its lighting was obviously inadequate.

So parts of the square were lit up. She stopped in her tracks. She returned to the stone bench in order to sit down, crossing her legs and rubbing her hands warmed her. Her back was still curved forward and her general appearance was pale and emaciated.

It was almost dawn. With the night so overcast a new cycle ought to begin. The neon sign was at the peak of its potency and, thrusting into the square's center, made itself more visible than ever.

She looked up at it, at the square and each one of her corners. She changed seats in order to position herself directly under a lamp. That way she was completely illuminated.

She picked up the paper bag that had accompanied her all
night long. It made a noise fom her handling, its opening was
crumpled and twisted as though sealed. She opened it carefully, took an ordinary pocket mirror from inside. She gazed at
her face for a long time, even practiced a smile. She repeatedly
passed her hand over her face. She brought the mirror up close
and drew it away. She gazed at herself from every possible
angle. At one point she leaned it against the edge of the nearby
railing in order to observe her face from the ground.

She stood up immediately walking toward the center. She
again exposed herself to the lighted sign. She gazed at her face
in the mirror, much more diluted and faintly crossed by the
lights there.

She returned to her original seat. She put the mirror away,
letting it fall into the paper bag. She dug her hand deep into
the bag and drew out a pair of scissors.

She raised her hand with the scissors toward her head. She cut
a tuft of her hair.

She stood up immediately.

She went to the center of the square and standing under the
eaves of light from the sign she started cutting her hair. Her
hair fell to the ground, covering the area around her. Her head
articulated rotary motions so that way her hands could reach
the nape of her neck, which was difficult for her. Her forehead
and shoulders were completely cleared and her hair was stuck
to the dome of her skull. She interrupted herself. She stroked
her hand caressingly over the nape of her neck, the front of her
head, the sides. She remained upright with her arms fallen and
the still half-open scissors in one hand. She breathed deeply.
Once again she raised her hands above her head and resumed
her uneven cutting. Her blanched skull showed through in bald
patches. The hollows of her cranium were evident. The parts
covered with hair were darker but still transparent. Generally
speaking, the uncropped parts were only half an inch or so
long. In spite of the cold, beads of sweat were running down
her brow. She stood upright a while longer in the center of the
square. Finally she walked toward one bench, picked up the

bag, and sat down on another that was under a lamp. She took out the mirror again. She put away the scissors. She gazed at herself, raising and tilting the mirror. For a moment it reflected the illuminated sign and even part of a branch of a tree. She took the scissors out of the bag again to go over one section of her forehead that was almost completely razed, because the hair would not disappear completely.

Dawn began to break weakly. A faint brightness competed, weakening the light from the streetlamps.

She changed places again toward a wooden bench and as she did so, her razed head turned gray once more. She sat there leaning her head against the back of the seat.

Dawn advanced rapidly, although the place still appeared in semidarkness. She remained seated with her head leaning against the back of the bench but her eyes were wide open.

The first cars began to swing by the square, their headlights still on.

Then across the way the first pedestrian walked by. Like the one from the night before, he walked briskly, with the lapels of his jacket turned up. One by one cars began following each other. The number of people passing by increased too as if magically multiplied by the natural light. She followed them with her gaze.

She also saw how a man came out of one of the houses, carefully locking the door behind him. Lights appeared in the windows of the apartment building. Noises began to flood the place.

Once again she searched in the bottom of the bag and took out a necklace of glass beads. She put it around her neck. The necklace fell over the front part of her dress.

That's how she remained, sitting erect on the seat with the paper bag in her hands. Her feet crossed on the ground. Her limpid face looking from side to side.

The first pedestrian crossed the square, certainly for the sake of the short cut.

Her absent-minded gaze focused on him vaguely, then openly. Their gazes crossed. She held the gaze for a moment, but then turned hers toward the street opposite. The crowd was mixed now, women, men, students. They were all going somewhere and now the noises grew louder just at the moment when the day became completely clear.

Extravag(r)ant and Un/erring Spirit

By Ronald Christ

> *The flash of a neon light split the night . . .*
> *And the sign flashed out its warning*
> *in the words that it was forming*
> *and the sign said . . .*
> *Animula, vagula, blandula . . .*
> *Quae nunc abibis in loca,*
> *Pallidula, frigida nundula . . . ?*

> Simon & Garfunkel + Hadrian

For centuries an image has measured mankind: a naked male figure centered in a square inscribed on a circle: *homo quadratus*, perhaps inspired by Villard de Honnecourt or Luca Pacioli and certainly depicted by Leonardo da Vinci: a man in a square, extending to a circle: a man squared and circled: a golden measure, a golden mean. Now, in her first novel, Diamela Eltit inserts into a different square a different figure, a female figure, one not golden, and if mean, then in that older sense of common, shabby. Once inserted, this new figure recovers ground we may not even have known to consider lost, invisible, for Eltit remarkably shows us not only the target of her vision but also composes the verbal optics by which that target is now sighted.

  A woman in the center of a public square circled by traffic, a measure of no one (except all those absent) yet adamantly, defiantly in that center, which also pinpoints her marginality of gender, her status in society: E. Luminata. Of course that's not her real name. In fact, she has no name, just as she has no personal history, no psychology, no *character* in short. She's pure literature, all letters. What may strike us first, though, is that whereas da Vinci's anonymous man bestrides the air within geometric frames so as to frame centered coordinates, the pseudonymous E. Luminata — named for the source of her naming — has vagabonded into the center of her circled square — thrust there by her author — to retake from the margins the center of that ruled page known as a public square and to claim — no: to *make* — a name for herself. To construct one with letters crossing her body as they are cast down by a neon advertisement overlooking that square. At Leonardo's ironic self-description: *uomo senza lettera*, this intruder upon her own territory might fling down her authentic pseudonymity, her virtual wish and will to be lettered, to be literate (literally), to write herself, to be written (on and of), to be writing and to *be* writing. At the same time, like so-called Vitruvian man, she has her existence in being seen; she is the multiple object of that self-conscious phenomenon notorious in our time: the *gaze*, under which she too spreads out, but mounted in neon butterfly hues ("pinning down her anatomical points"), extended to the limits of her scene.

And that's what she has: a scene, not a story. (That's what she is, too.) Eltit once explained:

> The book's protagonist is a female subject, the synthesis of the feminine with the lumpen. It takes place at night, during curfew, in an emptied space. She breaks the norms of nighttime to set up a curious spectacle with those who gain access to that place from their marginality: at one and the same time there results a contemplation of the surroundings and of a "contemplated being." There is also a recognition, an interaction, between her and the city. It's like the reappropriating of public space that had been arbitrarily usurped from us. Vagabonds are the only ones who dare to transgress there.[1]

The "curious spectacle" presents these nameless creatures, the lumpen — E. Luminata is lumpen too, errant, perhaps even arrant lumpen, but apart — gazing at her and she at them as she enacts her own baptism by immersing herself in the captured, lettered light, that technological water, which may spell a name for her. For she is the baptized, among other things. They are her celebrant audience, among other things. The sign, *el luminoso*, thrusting his sheaf of beams on her, printing, imprinting, her, is actively masculine; she, of course, female, so there is unremitting sexuality in the scene — at times as coarse as at others lyric —, a sexuality as venerable

---

[1]A.M.F., "Diamela Eltit: Acoplamiento incestuoso," *Hoy* 42 (12-18 August 1985): 41.

as the sun's penetrating the earth in agrarian myth; but this
scene is urban, these bundled shafts are artificial, pierce as
they may this contemporary non-saint in her gaping ecstacy: a
movie is being shot in the lit-up public square — another
contemplation, another observing gaze ("and the camera pulls
back and shoots the square in wide angle"). And if a movie, a
book as well, the one you read: set in type, proofed, printed,
trimmed by the binder's guillotine, folded, bound — "the book
displaying the illuminated sign that sells." But, caution: the
movie talk, the bookbinding terms, all the said-to-happen in
the book you read are means of narration, not necessarily
substantial with the narrated itself, whatever that may be: who
is interrogated, for example, is explicitly called into question,
as well as how Luminata "gives good account of herself" in all
the parts filmed or still-photographed in Section 5. The sound
of drab literalness — one way of narrating — in Section 10,
where no filming, no binding occur at all, confers no more
authority on its account than do the baroque torsions of
Section 3 on that account's (and character's) mutations. This
warning applies specially to those readers eager to construct
proportional analogies between elements in the narrative and
occurances in the world external to that narration; such
analogies more likely arise from the handling of the language
itself, including the punctuation: the dismemberment of Chile
embodied in the mutilation of sentence members.[2]

What these transgressors against the night have done
then, and she is chief among them in this, is convert illuminated darkness into signifying light. One might think: they
take back the night; another, following Norberg-Shulz, might
say: they turn a "non-place" into a "place"; [3] still another

---

[2] In 1977, in Santiago, while this novel was being written, Catalina Parra
exhibited among other works a long map of Chile severed in several places,
brutally stitched back together with red thread, and covered with medical
gauze. (Signs of wounds and medical interventions, including x-rays, were
frequent in non-official art during this period in Chile. Think of Lotty
Rosenfeld's photograph of Eltit in this novel.) When I asked Parra before the
show about the possibility of censorship, she in turn asked me how they could
censor a map, some thread, gauze. Similarly, how could they censor
punctuation in a novel? The theoretical cant of our day would explain that all
significance lies with the manipulated sign, not the signified.

[3] See Christian Norberg-Shulz, *Existence, Space and Architecture* (New York:
Praeger, 1971) and *"Meaning and Place" and Other Essays* (New York:
Academy, 1984).

might recall Góngora's *Solitudes*, with its hundreds of fiery
tongues, deniers of night, competitors with the sun and
feigners of daylight in deepest darkness:

> *Los fuegos — cuyas lenguas, ciento a ciento,*
> *desmintieron la noche algunas horas,*
> *cuyas luces, del sol competidoras,*
> *fingieron día en la tiniebla oscura. . . .* [4]

Someone else might proclaim: it's cinematic ("this landscape
is changed into day for night") like Eltit's work in video. And
all to the pounding beat, the banging, the battering of the
sign's intermittent penetration in the night, as well as to the
arrhythmic interruptions of the blows she inflicts on herself,
the impact of her multiple, repeated falls. The stamping,
galloping. The cuts. This is a violent scene.

Prior to its violence, though, it is a scene of infraction, to use the precise term of the book's best critic, Nelly
Richard.[5] Infraction *in* the scene itself: trespass in the blank
night of Pinochet's erasing curfew ("the rationality of a Chile
that halts its rhythm at night"); appropriation of space,
ironically of a "public" space, by an unrecognized public;
aggrandizement by seizing or attempting to seize the power of
naming: literally, the power to *denominate* as well as to
nominate oneself; inversion of order: edge over center, day
over night, outcast over ascendent. Infraction *by* the scene as
well: appropriation of narrative (instead, ten versions or
variations, verbal takes, of one sequence: "It was like a
circular scene rehearsed countless times"); trespass of genre:
incursions by drama, verse, film, lyric, epic, fragment — all
with that effect of formal rupturing we recognize as the

---

[4]Luis de Góngora, *Soledades* (Madrid: Alianza, 1982), 59: 687-690.

[5] In a paper, unpublished so far as I know: "Lumpérica o la desidentidad
(sobre una novela de Diamela Eltit)," March 1984, Richard reasonably and
minutely inventories the book's themes and techniques, unfashionably
rejecting any dramatization of either herself or her vocabulary. Subsequent
criticism has not attained a comparable analysis of the work's radicality — in
any sense of that word. Richard is also the author/editor of *Margins and
Institutions: Art in Chile Since 1973* (*Art & Text* 21), which provides the most
inclusive and thoughtful panorama of unofficial cultural expression during
Pinochet's rule and as such takes census for a combined social, political, and
aesthetic understanding of Eltit's novel.

novel's essential tradition, the anti-novel, starting with *Don Quixote* and cresting early in English with *Tristram Shandy* — as well as trespass of language: violation by breached syntax (inversion of order again), illicit grammar, vulgar and foreign speech, bastard spellings (cacography for calligraphy), dismembered syntax and diction. The text as invert. Thus, looking for the unofficial, for what contravenes the official in this novel, we may search the scene's action — minimally, illegal — and we must scrutinize its verbal presentation — maximally noncompliant:

I am interested in and continue to be excited by the ambiguity that can be generated by literary meanings, that opening displayed by some books in *cracking the monolith* of completed stories. I see myself seduced by certain micro-tales that attract to themselves innumerable gestures, rictus, and esthetic simulacra, that permit the *rebellious circulation of strategic fragments oppressed by official cultures.* The literary field where I find my calling — equally as producer and as reader — takes in fragmentariness and the superimposition of voices, views incompleteness, as well, as a narrative tactic, like a metaphor; I mean to say that it even views the strategy of strategy as the setting for writing, in an act of *liberating meanings and of protecting against the ideologizing of literature.*[6]

The text as resistance. ("A novel that tackles the theme of political nonconformity within a conservative literary canon may not result in criticism, precisely to the degree that its means of production remain untouched.")

A translation that tackles a novel of political and literary nonconformity within a conservative environment for translation (an environment where accolades can declare: "a rendering so good that you tend to forget that the poems were ever written in Spanish"[7]) may not result in criticism either, precisely to the degree that the translation's means of production, evidenced letter by letter in what you see before you on

---

[6] Diamela Eltit, "Quisiera," her speech accepting the José Nuez Martín Prize (Instituto de Letras de la Pontificia Universidad Católica de Chile: November 1995). My emphases. María Ester Martínez kindly furnished me with a copy of the speech.

[7] James Dickey's blurb for the third edition of John Frederick Nims's translation of *The Poems of St. John of the Cross* (Chicago: University of Chicago Press, 1995). My thanks to Carol Maier for this example of an all-too-usual formulation.

the page, remain untouched. That virgin intacta of invisible
translation has not been invited to this conjugal celebration,
this sacrilegious baptism, this *via dolorosa* of Eltit's novel in
English; instead, I have invited myself, as I now invite you, *to
participate* in Eltit's engagement with language, *to recover* it,
approximatively, in our own — to partake of an *engagé*
translation of an *engagé* novel, though in senses that Sartre's
term was never meant to embrace.[8] In other words, for us to
join in the artisanal disconformity of Eltit's novel as activa-
tors, not observers, and to issue that work in our language. No
mirror up to literature, then, no transparent eyeball trained
upon the foreign, and certainly no magic switch trick; no, still
yet another gaze, this time from English. That's the goal.

To achieve that goal, I joined in Eltit's disjointing
("phobia *d* is/members"); her inversions and displacements
("and sweating her opulent backside shimmying from all the
effort"); her special effects, such as cinematic, synechdotal
close up, which matches her verbal fragmentariness with the
visual ("The part of her face that modulates — I'm thirsty —
is shot in close-up"); her neologisms and spoken collisions
("thinflamation of the bitch/ thinfection of those mutts"); her
grammatical insubordinations ("who on offers herself"). Into
each such "event" in her prose, as Kenneth Burke would
rightly have termed them,[9] I entered with a mission to partici-

---

[8] The term "invisible" I take from Lawrence Venuti's general discussion in
The Translator's Invisibility (London and New York: Routledge, 1995). I was
introduced to this provocative and, to me, unexceptionable study by Carol
Maier, from whom I borrow the italicized terms as well as the phrase
"engagement with language": Carol Maier, "Recovering, Re-covering, and the
Translation of Work by Rosa Chacel and María Zambrano," in selected though
as yet unpublished conference proceedings (April 1994).

[9] For example, in *Counter-Statement* (Berkeley: University of California
Press, 1968), 134, Burke writes:

Some writers, who seek 'conversational' rather than 'written; effects,
apparently conceive of the sentence as a totality; they ignore its internal
relationships almost entirely, preferring to make each sentence as homogeneous as a piece of string. By such avoidance of logical grouping they do
undeniably obtain a simple fluency which, if one can delight in it sufficiently,
makes every page of Johnson a mass of absurdities — but their sentences are,
as sentences, uneventful.

Eltit, whose effects are both 'conversational' and 'written' cuts the string,
shreds it, knots up the "homogenous," and is nowhere simply fluent except to
complex effect.

pate and recover, but overall and more generally important, I
sought to retake the eventfulness of Eltit's syntax in register-
ing these events in the sum of their variation, fragmentation,
fluctuation — in the syntax's deliberate alienation of reading's
comfy complacency. The distancing I sought I took from
Eltit's Spanish; I lay English upon her Spanish, not as upon
the rack but as upon an armature, adjusting willfully, adminis-
tering a not always fixed, not always benign chiropractic to the
language's syntactic spine.

Where possible — and possible for me in my English
is all I mean — I follow the book's rigor ("a word, another
word, that exact unique word, the page"), heeding the syntax,
reiterating among the determined lexicon. Yet what Eltit builds
is a widening, changeful network of meanings and connections
from these "exact words," so that a simple English-for-
Spanish exchange, if such were possible, would not do. As one
engaged, I try to recover the engagement with the nexus but
not to imitate its terms strictly. *Slavishly* is the revealing,
absent modifier here; instead, I am a willing, *eager* participant, which raises a point of some interest: writers looking at
the translation uniformly remarked the repetition of words,
uniformly suggested an enriching variation. Eltit's apparent
poverty, however, reflects not the limits of some *arte povera*,
but a wealth her novel earns, much as Borges stated differently, in a differing context, when he said: "I have already
conquered my poverty: among thousands, I have recognized
the nine or ten words that accord with my spirit. . . ."[10]
Resistance to this opportunity for variation, a vow of poverty
of sorts, within a book that richly varies itself, characterizes
Eltit's effort. We tend to think, admiringly, of resistance as
enacted from the bottom up; we might also reflect,
judgmentally, on that Spanish dictator said to have pro-
claimed: "To govern is to resist." Authors, Eltit herself, are
different dictators, sayers, governors of words. Her gover-
nance resisted still another — deadly — outside as well as
inside her book.

This insistent repeating of certain words — among
them *cross, crack, bristle, erect, stumble* — signals Eltit's
resolve not to swerve, not *to err*, in the diction of her novel;

---

[10] Jorge Luis Borges, "Profesión de fe literaria," *El Tamaño de mi esperanza*
(Buenos Aires: Proa, 1926), 153.

but they do not resolve into *leitmotivs*: they are architectural
elements of the structure she is erecting — a book, a book
within or of the book ("They arrange themselves like lines
ordered on the page and every inch of the square imprints
them and every drop of the rain inks them"), a structure of
person and place — and should be read as textual/textural
reoccurrences that accumulate meaning, much the way
brushstrokes accumulate color in one of Fantin-Latour's
paintings as described to him by Whistler:

But you know I prefer the composition of the other work — not you
understand only the painted objects nor even the arrangement of them
— but the composition of the colours which for me is true colour —
and this is how it seems to me first of all that, with the canvas as
given, the colours should be so to speak *embroidered* on it — in other
words the same colour reappearing continually here and there in the
same way a thread appears in an embroidery — and so on with the
others — more or less according to their importance — the whole
forming in this way an harmonious pattern — Look how the
Japanese understand this! They never search for contrast, but on the
contrary, they're after repetition. . . .[11]

By insisting on their resolute reappearance, Eltit weaves a taut
fabric in which her exerted force on repeated words, crammed
into unusual contexts, bid to new uses, unites differences as it
mobilizes meaning. *Cross*, for example: people cross the
square; gazes cross; the protagonist does not cross with, as
mongrels do, nor is she crossed; the sign's letters cross bodies
in the square; she crosses the pavement with her chalked
letters.[12] Sometimes the repeated words rise almost

[11] Translation of Whistler's letter to Henri Fantin-Latour (30 September 1868), *Whistler on Art: Selected Letters and Writings of James McNeill Whistler*, ed. Nigel Thorp (Washington, D.C.: Smithsonian, 1994), 33, 35. Compare, from *E. Luminata's* first sentence: " . . . that woman who recroses her own face, incessantly appliquéd. . . ."

[12] The cross motif has been extended by Lotty Rosenfeld, a collaborator with Eltit as well as a participant in the dialogue that the author mentions in her preface to this volume. Rosenfeld's photograph of Eltit's face projected onto a façade, part of a joint project with Eltit, appeared on the novel's original cover. See Richard, *Margins and Institutions*, 57-60, for Rosenfeld's *Una milla de cruces sobre el pavimento* (A Mile of Crosses on the Pavement) as well as Eltit's essay by the same title (Santiago, Chile: CADA, 1980); also see *Desacato: Sobre la obra de Lotty Rosenfeld* (Santiago de Chile: Zegers, 1986), especially Eltit's essay "Desacatos."

unnoticeably ("Some red lines crossed her dress"), other times
they are enforced, contriving a connection ("her head stumbles
so far forward") so that *crossing + stumbling*, for example,
emerges in structural and related elements, like brushstrokes,
bricks, and gradually marshals meaning ("a word, another
word . . . ; the slowness with which meanings become organized"). Picking out the thread of *crossing*, we may come to
see the novel's words gradually organizing an order or a theme
or subject of confrontational intermingling: *mestizaje*, blood
crossed and mixed in forms historical, cultural, individual; just
as the novel's terms cross forms traditional, generic, and
lexical. In other words, the novel's meaning resides in its
meshing and dismembering of its own verbal and syntactic
elements, its own insistent fusion and dispersion, as much as
in what those elements represent; so that since Eltit's reach
extends so far as the impacted inventions of Joyce's *Finnegans
Wake* ("Thsight near left me eyes when I seen her put thounce
otay ithpot," "Lumpsome is who lumpsum pays") those same
collisions justify translated phrases such as "thinflammation of
the bitch/ thinfection of those mutts."[13] Her grasp also includes
that territory mapped by Arguedas's *Deep Rivers*, where
Quechua and Spanish collide and combine, as well as Vallejo's
savage rendings and rivetings.

The fusion and dispersion in Eltit's language, the
membering and dismembering, begins as early as her book's
title, which, in the original (*Lumpérica*) fuses the German
lumpen, a word perhaps more usual in Spanish, where Marxist
terminology is commonplace, than in current American
English, and *perica*, which denotes everything from babe and
chick to an undetermined person, a sort of boulevard Jane
Doe, a prostitute too: a walker of the streets who may also be a
streetwalker. She is one of the *stellae errantes*. A *Traviata*, for
our time, different, but still tra-*via*-ta — *sola, abbandonata*
too. She is a synthesis, Eltit tells us, and the author's title
proposes such a synthesis, so that title, too, must be translated,
its constructed nature, bearing on the novel's method and
meaning, reinscribed; yet, since such constructions can rarely
pass beyond their linguistic borders under the same identity,
the title, too, had to be naturalized, in this case first becoming
a synthesis of *lumpen* and *errata*, with an accent displaced

---

[13] James Joyce, *Finnegans Wake* (New York: Viking, 1962), 262, 270.

from Spanish usage. Then, because there appeared to be no escaping the ugly thud of *lump* in pronouncing that title, I compromised, using the character's name: *E. Luminata*.

Even in *Lumperráta* there was something lost in the translation, notably the overtones of *(Am)erica*, which are specially dear — no surprise — to Americans, North Americans that is (though the author claims never to have considered that resonance); but there was also something found: by transferring the verbal coincidence from the *p* to the *e*, I was able to inherit a largely disinherited vagabond/vagrant theme articulated in the chain *err, error, errant (arrant), erratic, errata*—all summed in *aberrant*. That trial title gone, the series still veins the novel, another testimony to Dennis Dollens's accurate assertion that this book is an ideal candidate for hypertextual presentation.

E. Luminata is not only a translation of the novel's title but of the character's title as well. I translate her name so as to make it coincide with the English sound of the informing *illuminate*. In other words, I aim to translate, where I can, effects as well as meanings, rhetorical devices as well as lexical significations. Among those devices: the splicing punctuation, which, by articulating splits, joins ("a city reconstituted/ out of some operetta"); the comma-splicing punctuation that couples by putting casters on clauses, that omits syntactical signals in favor of rhetorical punctuation: signs of emphasis and effect, that, like most else in the book, culture the ambiguity of more than one reading ("But the writings open to more than one interpretation occurred there").

Mestizaje in the language, then; but also in the ignored peoples of the book and precisely in the collapsed Mapuche hut or *ruka*, whose architecture, structure is the extruded effort of the protagonist's own self ("It is her structure that is close to falling"), a commingling that isolates and brings down the primary, reduces it to the ground but also responds to the striving upward ("Those others appear opaque and reduced; she in contrast is constructed"). We need to recall as well that the *machi*, the female shaman of the Auracanians, who is figured in Section 4.6 traditionally mounts a raised platform to enter her trance ("Machi/ the mater healer towers up for the mutts").

The related, sometimes simultaneous though never identical, rising and reduction thus informs the book, and may remind us of the Inca's subjection of neighboring societies, as the Inca Garcilaso writes over and over, themselves only to be reduced utterly by the Spaniards.[14] The Incas, however, as Sara Castro-Klarén reminds me, and the Inca Garcilaso repeatedly states and other modern scholars affirm, "respected the religion, language and other customs of the peoples conquered and superimposed their rule on them."[15] Therefore we must distinguish between reduction by Spanish conquest and the assimilation imposed by the Incas. As Marica and Robert Asher report from Pedro Cieza de León's book published in 1553:

> . . . *Cieza thought of the Incas as victims . . . ; as he says: "wherever the Spanish have passed, conquering and discovering, it is as though a fire had gone, destroying everything it passed." . . . The Incas moved upon a group as if they were the bearers of important gifts. A deity bringing better times, or a method to make the land more fruitful, or food if the need for it existed, are examples of the gifts. If the gifts were accepted, there was no need for violence; if not, force was applied. In any case, the gifts were delivered, and thus, selected parts of Inca culture were everywhere superimposed. According to Cieza, the Incas did not want to destroy and replace the cultures alredy there.*[16]

---

[14] The word appears and reappears in Garcilaso's *Comentarios Reales* like one of the threads in Eltit's fiction; for one example: "Desde Llauantu envió el gran Túpac Inca Yupanqui parte de su ejército a la conquista y *reducción* de una provincia llamada Muyupampa. . . . Pasados algunos años en estos ejercicios de paz, volvió el Inca a la conquista de las provincias que había al norte, que llaman Chinchasuyu, por *reducirla*[s] a su Imperio. . . . (*Comentarios Reales*, Mexico: Porrúa, 1990, 334, 336; emphasis mine.) Eltit's knowledge and use of the *Commentaries* is well established; for example, see Djelal Kadir, *The Other Writing* (West Lafayette, IN: Purdue, 1993), 193-194, as well as her interview in *Hoy* 42, where she speaks about reading in the Incan traditions, from which she took the name of one of her characters in *Por la patria.*

With no euphemism at all, modern anthroplopogists use the word *reduction* to refer to contemporary Araucanian reservations.

[15] Sara Castro-Klarén, letter to the author (undated).

[16] Marcia Asher and Robert Asher, *Code of the Quipu, A Study in Media, Mathematics, and Culture* (Ann Arbor: University of Michigan Press, 1981), 3-5. The Ashers, to whose work I was directed by Sara Castro-Klarén, quote Cieza in Harriet de Onis's translation (Victor Wolfgang von Hagen, ed., *The Incas of Pedro de Cieza de León* (Norman: University of Oklahoma Press, 1959).

Inevitably, these reductions result in a connected element in the book's organization: the *fall* (directly related to *stumble*). The scenes of E. Luminata's fall are multiple (Section 9), the light falls, the clapboard falls, the credits fall, signs of the indigenous culture fall. Linking the terms explicitly, as the novel seldom does, we may say that in the crossing there has been a fall and that Eltit's, E. Luminata's effort is to erect, to tower again: "from sheer willpower another structure is erected."

The fall is first alluded to by the squinting reference to an indigenous culture reduced by the Greeks ("Peltasgiant"), then again in the central climax of Section 4, where the Araucanian dwelling, constructed by force of imagination, falls ("the thatched ruka topples"): E. Luminata, like Diamela Eltit in this book, is a threatened builder ("When one lives in a world that is collapsing, constructing a book perhaps may be one of the few survival tactics"). Forces on the construction, then, are oppositional, all coefficient, all countervailing:

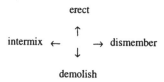

It is a risky construction (written in risky constructions): "towering up" and "toppling," even "boggedangling" in a setting of "so much of the city of Santiago reduced to grass." As edifice, the book itself threatens to topple on account of its fragmentedness, its irregularity, but in fact it towers as the substantive and technical hybridization binds seemingly scattering elements ("mixing voices, electronically"). The reader participates, reconstructing the book by making such connections, sometimes arduously; and the translator precedes the reader in such participation by preserving or displacing them. For example of the latter: looking at each other, people are not said, in English, to be crossing eyes; their gazes, however, may be so described. So: the networks are here, but not accountable to the reviewer's habitual system of double-entry bookkeeping in which any item in column "A" (Spanish: *ojos*) must correspond linearly to an item in column "B" (English: *gaze*), the latter typically criticized as debit. (One persevering thread, the repeated variations on *golpe* [*strike, blow*, but also, and pertinently, *coup* as in *coup d'etat*], does not stitch the English text, and this is indeed a loss, especially since the English-language reader will rarely have had the experience to feel fully the burden of Eltit's indirections: the "rationality" of urban night without the usual people abroad, the cop cars patrolling, the unending interrogations of innocent actions with inhuman results ["interrogation here is a sacred word"], the reduction of Santiago to a glitzy wasteland, "a city reconstituted/ out of some operetta," with pasteboard guardsmen, no doubt, and sham delights — all signs of the military regime's murderous, mystifying power. As a matter of plain fact, I witnessed some of that desolate phantasmagoria. I have undergone, then and there, here and elsewhere, now and still — other inquisitions as well; without physical threat and without the purgatorial duration of the interrogations in the novel, to be sure, yet with sufficient peril to self and work, and mostly in my own county — and that lucent grayness of the peopleless night in public places, a scrim of lucidly barren order between one and the visible world, does not let me forget how *realistic* the fantastic scene in this book truly is.) On the other and lesser hand, substitutions, such as *square* for *plaza*, permit that sole setting to be *squared* and *gridded* in English in order to be *lined, ordered, ruled* — think of it: *ruled*! — like the page that both Eltit and E. Luminata write. For certain things lost in translation others may be found. Still, and finally: let there be no doubts: Spanish, Eltit's Spanish, cannot be slipped inside English, my English, like a supple hand within an amenable glove. Translation provokes intransigencies, and it should respect them; a transit should not be forced. So, for example, the triple word play on *bacchanal* (*vac/a-nal*) remains here in its doubly hyrbrid nature, illuminating language from within, as my best try, *bac/k/ine-(a)nal*, would not have done.

Given the debased currency of official cultural dialogue at the time she was writing, Eltit boldly embezzled language, and a loyal translator — I do not mention fidelity — will try to replicate her transgression. There are limits though.

Eltit can and does consistently invert, sometimes contorts word order, insistently that of subject and verb, whereas English is a subject-first language with a less flexible spine, so I suggest the presence of such deviance (another name for style) without recovering its instances one by one. Eltit — she says so herself — takes shelter in any ambiguity: the possessive *su*, for one small example, which may stand for *her, his, its, their, your* (singular as well as plural) in Spanish, often wobbles uncertainly among those choices in her text, whereas English usually requires specificity. (When constrained to specify myself, I have sometimes asked Eltit to do so too: a humiliation for my hopes, since even native speakers I've consulted disagreed — as they ought to have done.) Working this ambiguity still harder, she pointedly con-fuses the feminine protagonist and the square ("She's really coming across, that square") in their role as recipient of the sign's unrelenting blows. She effects another destabilizing wobble by pointing sense in two directions across syntactic divides and by compressing:

She conceals her womb opens

                        fetus and figure expand in the quadrant's holes

which suggests how the pilgrim may occasionally stumble to his profit, stumped though he may be: "she conceals" refuses to stand alone, and "opens" seems to contradict "conceals," so retrace your steps:

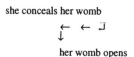

where the syntax has lapped "her womb" into simultaneous subject and object — a condition of reciprocal gaze and a coincidence of signs different only in order of magnitude from that in the book's title or "she moo/s/hears." Then, having read forward: "fetus and figure expand," read back so that fetus and figure open up her womb, cause following effect:

→ → → → → → →
She conceals her womb opens
           ↓ ↑
                fetus and figure expand in the quadrant's
                ← ← ← ← ← ← ← ←

Eltit mulls her syntax, which may be properly termed synaptic, as well as her vocabulary, mullions them with slashes and gaps too. There are intermittencies in her lines. Above, the syntax is mixed, fused; at other times the author disperses her lines in literally deranged arrangement:

> . . . She pulls out her best bits

> and catalogues them in her labors/

> she seeks them delicately

> la tan sua

> in order to charm them

> — it's part of her job —

which underscores the line as unit of meaning in much of this book — a condition of verse. And, it is true that Eltit's prose is apparitional, apparitionally verse, much of the time; yet it is apparitionally impure prose as well; nor should we read for these states hermaphroditic prose poetry; no, but prose reordered to varying conditions of verse, and poetic elements towed under by the power of prose both everyday and elevated and almost always susceptible to comprehension by reading aloud. If in Section 3 the lines do not scan, if a nearly imperceptible metrical stretch is an ever-weakening pulse, prolonged, arrhythmia itself, that is nevertheless the spell of Góngora and *culteranismo* weaving in the background. The baroque master's description of a fisherman's intricate net, a knotty labyrinth, emblematizes Eltit's novel:

> *Fábrica escrupulosa, y aunque incierta*
> *siempre murada, pero siempre abierta.*

> (Fine-made fabric, and though changeable
> ever walled, yet ever open wide)[17]

---

[17] Góngora, "Soledad Segunda," 90: 77-80. *Incierta* is a recurring word in Góngora, as it is in Eltit, and in its positive senses of *uncertain* or *changeable*, not *indecisive* or *irresolute*, it is key for both writers.

And his practice of writing one word, then the same exact, unique word for another thing — *snow*, famously, for all things white and blank, but also all such things for snow — may be seen as like Eltit's (but then, indigenous languages of her continent, Quechua for instance, often impressed an identical word for multiple service, to the incomprehension of the Spaniards, as the Inca Garcilaso explains).[18] Góngora, too, has been called obscure, "unreadable" — gloriously so —, like Joyce in our time. It is a risk that Eltit takes, that this translation takes as well: obscurity, which functions here in the double sense that Higginson remarked to Emily Dickinson, another taker of valuable risks: "Though obscurity is sometimes, in Coleridge's phrase, a compliment to the reader, yet it is never safe to press this compliment too hard."[19] But this is not a safe book, nor was it meant to be; it is disobedient. Góngora's, Joyce's, Eltit's works are "writerly," not "readerly," as Roland Barthes would have said, and the translator must take a stand with the writer or the reader but not against either. Eltit has considered her position in this relationship:

Of course I conceive of the literary as a multiple field of options and practices. I am a great admirer of the great literary tradition in Spanish, especially of medieval literature and the amazing baroque; and, at the same time, I feel my relation to those literatures in which language and meaning share a privileged space of unfolding and folding up, in play not exempt from opacity and mystery. I do think about the reader. I sense the reader as an accomplice of the text, as a performer of the task of unraveling; that is, I can only imagine the act of reading as an adventure in which the most important thing is venturing and in venturing to be venturesome.[20]

Customarily, translators comfort readers along their way; indeed, they pamper readers, removing the stumbling blocks, rendering the adventurous easefully disadventurous.

---

[18] For example, in Chapter 4 of the Second Book, he states: "This error arose precisely because the Spaniards did not know the many and varied meanings of the word *huaca*. . . . ." (*Comenatrios Reales*, 54). Garcilaso's next chapter is headed: "About the Many Other Things the Word *Huaca* Means."

[19] T. W. Higginson, "Emily Dickinson's Letters," *Atlantic Monthly* 68 (October 1891): 44-56.

[20] Diamela Eltit, "Quisiera."

Translators have much been explainers as well as fillers-in and smoothers-out and adders-on. Given Eltit's evident, principled decision not to coddle readers, I decided to translate that decision into English, on principle, in respect. Given Eltit's cited rootedness in the baroque and Eltit's explicit testimony to that style in her novel, a style of which Borges risked the definition: "[T]he baroque is that style which deliberately exhausts (or seeks to exhaust) its possibilities and borders on its own caricature,"[21] I have deliberately sought to deliver the translation to an equal or nearly equal limit. Thus, the text's derangement is verbatim; so is the character's: "She has disorganized language." The recrudescence in English of what Barthes would have labeled Eltit's, Luminata's "enigmatic disorganization" is bona fide.[22] The reader will do well to keep in mind Severo Sarduy's dictum: "Writing is the art of disorganizing an order and organizing a disorder" (as well as its corollary: "Writing is the art of patchwork").[23]

Which means that here you may take satisfaction in the toppling of conventional orders and the erecting of nonconformist structures. You will have to re-read as you read, and activated that way you may gain a sense that you are reading a translation. Good, so far as that leads you to participating in a recovery of Eltit's achieved resistance. Her

---

[21] Jorge Luis Borges, *Historia universal de la infamia* (Buenos Aires: Emecé, 1962), 9. John Barth insightfully appropriates the notion in relation to modern literature; see his "The Literature of Exhaustion," *The Friday Book* (New York: Putnam, 1984).

[22] Recall Barthes: "In *S/Z*, an opposition was proposed: *readerly/writerly*. A readerly text is one I cannot write (can I write today like Balzac?); a *writerly* text is one I read with difficulty, unless I completely tranform my reading regime. I now conceive . . . that there may be a third textual entity . . . something like the *receivable*. The receivable would be the unreaderly text which catches hold, the red-hot text, a product continuously outside any likelihood and whose function — visibly assumed by its *scriptor* — would be to contest the mercantile constraint of what is written; this text, guided, armed by a notion of the unpublishable, would require the following response: I can neither read nor write what you produce, but I *receive* it, like a fire, a drug, an enigmatic disorganization." (*Roland Barthes* by Roland Barthes, trans. Richard Howard [New York: Hill and Wang, 1977]), 54. Obviously Eltit goes not so far as the unpublishable, the unreadable, but she resolves in that direction, with a stated intent "to contest the mercantile constraint of what is written." I thank William Vesterman for recalling me to this passage.

[23] Severo Sarduy, *Cobra*, trans. Suzanne Jill Levine (New York: Dutton, 1975), 10, 14.

Spanish, either, can't be judged by that outworn standard: "Did you ever hear anybody talk like that?" Which also means, as I've indicated, that you will sacrifice a tattered standard of translation: its self-effacement. Eltit's lowly but not humble empress is complicatedly clothed in her simplicity, and you can't take your eyes off those remnants and rags and riches; the translation's, less riveting, no less avoid your stare.

      Another sort of doubling or folding, the compounded angles of vision, further characterizes the novel as *ekphrasis*, a verbal representation of an imagined work of visual art, but with the term's modern inflection toward the process of the artwork's coming into being: in this case, the movie in the process of being shot, this book in the process of being made. Yet, note how the terminology of film impinges glancingly, erratically on the novel, as do other many of its other devices. Consider also: in explaining how her break with novelistic form constantly put her at risk of not being able to go on writing, Eltit has affirmed: "Therefore I had the urgent need to come up with the means for going on, and I incorporated the cinematic as a device that would allow me to get from one page to another."[24] Thus, a parallel with Nabokov, in which one of his "heroes" corresponds to the cinematic in Elitit and his different "ways" to her formal variations from section to section as well as within sections, may prove useful:

[T]he heroes of the book are what can be loosely called "methods of composition." It is as if a painter said: look, here I'm going to show you not the painting of a landscape, but the painting of different ways of painting a certain landscape, and I trust their . . . fusion will disclose the landscape as I intend you to see it.[25]

Thus, too, another parallel with Joyce may also prove useful: just as his Homeric schema served Joyce better for organizing his writing of *Ulysses* than it does us for organizing a reading his novel, so in Eltit's case, the cinematic element furthers her narrating more than her narration. Because of each writer's

[24] Guillermo García-Corales, "Entrevista con Diamela Eltit: una reflexión sobre su literatura y el momento político-cultural chileno," *Revista de Estudios Colombianos* 9 (1990): 74.

[25] Vladimir Nabokov, *The Real Life of Sebastian Night* (New York: New Directions, 1941), 95.

skill, however, the specific technique is blended as its own strand in the respective novels — like a successful *ficelle* in one of Henry James's fictions — and the reader must exercise due discretion. In Section 10, for example, which many readers find the most summary of the novel's entire action as well as the most explicit, all that stand in for elaborations of cinematography in other sections are the electric lighting and that hand mirror that E. Luminata leans upright, against a support, so as to catch a glimpse of herself. (The mirror's truncated view may also confirm the oddly singular "branch of the tree" that reoccurs throughout the narration.)

Consequently the translation reflects the technical vocabulary of movies as another means to furtherance of the gaze itself, not as an established jargon. And allusions to other works, another sustaining means, similarly re-emerge fragmentarily, askew. Thus when E. Luminata plunges her hand into the fire ("like a quotation"), thereby evoking Mucius (afterward called Scaevola or Lefthanded, whom Livy recorded as losing his right hand in the original of her act of loyal defiance[26]), it is E. Luminata's *left* hand that sinks into the flames; and when she utters the film's one speech, quoted directly and repeatedly, she reiterates the fifth of Christ's Seven Last "Words" but in ordinary, everyday Spanish, like a modern translation of John's Gospel: "I'm thirsty," aboriginated in Psalm 69: 21: "Yea, they put poison in my

---

[26] See Titus Livius, *Livy*, Books I and II, trans. B. O. Foster (Cambridge, MA: Loeb, 1948), 256-261. Gaius Mucius Scaevola, of his own volition, crossed into the enemy camp with the goal of slaying Porsinna, the Etruscan king laying siege to Rome. Mistaking a secretary for the king, Mucius stabbed the wrong man with his sword and was apprehended as he strode away. Brought before the king, he famously declared: "I am a Roman citizen; men call me Gaius Mucius. I am your enemy, and as an enemy I would have slain you; I can die as resolutely as I could kill: both to do and to endure valiantly is the Roman way." Terrified by his vulnerability and furious at the same time, Porsinna ordered Mucius cast into a sacrificial fire, whereat Mucius exclaimed: "'*En tibi ut sentias quan vile corpus sit ils que magnam gloriam vident,' destramque accenso ad sacridicium foculo inicit.*'": "'Look, that you may see how cheap they hold their bodies whose eyes are fixed upon renown! [and he] thrust his hand into the fire that was kindled for the sacrifice." Seeing Mucius's hand burn "as if his spirit were unconscious of sensation, the king was almost beside himself with wonder."

Elements of this whole scene, not only the dramatic burning, illuminate Eltit's scene: the stealing into the enemy camp under darkness, the stabbing, the citizen's valor, the sacrificial fire, the immolation, the beholder's wonder — not least of all that key phrase in her original: *vile corpus.*

food,/ And gave me vinegar to drink for my thirst."[27] (Later, the section entitled "Quo vadis" follows a similar principle of colloquial and gestural quotation, being self-translated to "Where you going?"; and of course "sometimes there may surface one of the famous quotations," one of the others, that is, like the historical and and literary allusions, ranging from Julius Caesar to Mallarmé.[28]) This passional element, these stations secular and sacred ("the libidinous old hag, . . . the forsaken woman" *and* the long *via dolorosa, via crucis* (the injured "soles of her feet, . . . the garment, the veil, . . . the crown of thorns"), the multiple scenes of falls, which echo the Falls of Christ, a medieval imitative devotion in turn translated into the Stations of the Cross in the 16th and17th century,[29] the eucharist of the chalk ("hands each one a bit of chalk she is breaking between her fingers"; "Only the very tip of their fingers touch the bit of chalk.") — all these elements make of the square a church, of her movments an imitative ritual, not only Christian: when the *machi*, the Araucanian shamaness, is just about to fall to the ground, senseless, she begins to spin on

---

[27] The Psalms, *The Complete Bible, an American Translation*, ed. Edgar J. Goodspeed (Chicago: University of Chicago Press, 1939), 535.

[28] Although she does not cite specific allusions, Eugenia Brito has given the best account of Eltit's responsiveness to Mallarmé, especially to his notions of the page. See *Campos minados: literatura post-golpe en chile*: (Santiago de Chile: Cuarto Propio, 1994).

[29] Variously numbered over the centuries, the Falls and the Last Words are sometimes seven in number but, like most else in the novel, they appear selectively, fractionally. With the general codification of the *Via Sanctis* in the 16th century, the falls were reduced to three: Stations III, VII, and IX; and this devotion of the primitive Church became a popular metaphor and theme, reflected in diverse works that use the Three Falls as a metonymy for the Passion itself, such as Manuel Cayetano Parrales y Guerrero, *Las tres caidas que dió la magestad de Cristo en el camino del Monte Calvario: puestas a la consideración de las almas devotas para que la mediten* [Christ's Three Falls on the Road to Calvary: Placed before the Consideration of Devout Souls for Meditation] (Mexico: Viuda de Joseph Bernado de Hogal, 1753). That the devotion and the image remain a popular representation into our own century may be gathered from Santiago Guerra's reconstruction of the oral text *Las tres caídas de Jesucristo* (performed in Ixtapalapa, Mexico City, on Holy Thursday, April 1945; Mexico: Universitaria, 1947, volume 6 of the Mexican Folklore Society). Besides Christ's falls, it would be appropriate, in the context of Eltit's novel, to recall Mary's swoon into supporting arms, which figures in the iconography of the Deposition and may inform Luminata's interrupted fall in the novel.

her own axis, and a male crosses over to her in order to
support her and prevent her fall, just as the unamed man is
accused of doing in the novel's two interrogations.[30] All these
elements also introduce into the novel another sort of
ekphrasis, the progress of performance art, both sacred and
profane, threading it with a spectacular indomitability, both
authorial and fictive, triumphant and demolished ("the public
square from wretched to sublime"). No wonder that E.
Luminata, like Cluny's ambiguous, encircled Unicorn, another
Christ/Virgin figure, is "sole desire" among lumpen.

But she herself is not sole. Still another view, another
fusion emerges in the dialogue, visual and verbal, between
narrating persona and protagonist: the erotic litanies ("and my
madonna lips suck her madonna breast longingly") are one
example, the identity of uttered and quoted words not in
quotations another: "I am thirsty (in the square) I am freezing
(in the square)"; and when we come in this quilted tale upon
"Her Remnants," we reach a seamed and seamlessly bio-
graphical (if not strictly factual) merging of protagonist as
character and narrator, not a simple identification but a
contrived hybridization, like that in the book's fused words:

Between the years of her birth and death she was able/
to limit herself to three occupations. These being conditioned by
historic events that determined incidents by appearances.
During those years she divided herself between fiction and the fiction
of her occupations. That way she succeeded in striking a balance
among the fiction desired by externals, another she did not recognize
as such and that resulting from both. This last she designated her
own.

These divisions, which John Nagle points out may recall
Mary's as Virgin, Mother, and Mourner, also correspond to
what we loosely, vulgarly, but comprehendingly, call schizoid,
and they also correspond to comparable ones in the character/
narration of E. Luminata, the I/me that Elit extracts from the
Indian word *Inche* ("and my madonna face looking into her
madonna face"). What is whose, who is what, precisely and
broadly though specifically considered, are questions that

---

[30] See Alfred Métraux, "Le Shamanisme araucan," *Revista del Instituto de
Antropología de Tucumán*, II, 10 (1942), 337. Métraux's article is an excellent
basis from which to consider the shamanisitic ritual in Eltit's novel.

drive this novel. Having inflicted burns and cuts on her own arms, it was Eltit, after all, whose face was being projected onto that wall across the street from the brothel where she read from this novel during the course of a collaborative "art action" entitled *Maipu* — in the process being photographed, the photograph then being reproduced on her novel's original cover. It is Eltit's face, too, that looks out at us in Section 8. Luminata's bright dark night of the soul is Eltit's too.[31] We read their text, both their texts, slashed with virgules, just as we look at it, punctuated with gashes in the photograph also recording the dress rehearsal. Everywhere the book is marked with the female's sign, the woman's cut — virga both divina and censoria.

Mucius/Luminata's ambidexterity in the fire scene thus underscores the novel's established ambiguity, no where more evident than in its various mutilations. If the protagonist's flesh is cut, if the author's image itself appears with slashed arms, words are severed too ("her ma lady man ual"), yet their disjointing is also their recoupling ("lumpenluminated"); and in like paradox the book's humiliations, like those of an earlier book, are glories: we do well to read none of its signs one way only; on these pages there is neither meaning nor direction that corresponds to either a *sentido único* or a *sens unique*. Remark E. Luminata's self-shearing. Interpreted as various self-abnegations, the protagonist's cropping her hair with those scissors she carries along with a pocket mirror in a paper bag — after all, this book is "the construction of a transitory narrative that takes as its model a ragged bag lady" —, her cropping is dedication as well: think of Joan of Arc, think of Mme. Falconetti! It is also grooming, a kind of negative decoration. (That *shearing, cropping, grooming* all bear connotations of the animal world is to the point and shows how Eltit's accumulative method carries across into the system of English.) The complex signification of E. Luminata's act emerges when placed alongside another "original," less obvious though neither less warranted nor less intricate in intertwined submission/ domination:

---

[31] See Nelly Richard, *Margins and Institutions*, 66-73.

The Mark of Favor Bestowed by the Inca on his People

The Inca Manco Cápac busied himself with such and similar tasks for many years, all for the good of his subjects; and having come to know their fidelity, the love and the respect with which they served him, the devotion they paid him, he wanted to ennoble them with titles and insignia like those he himself bore upon his head. All this came after his persuading them that he was indeed the Sun's offspring, so that they would esteem his favor even more highly and be still further beholden to him. Consequently, it is known that the Inca Manco Cápa and all his descendants after him, in imitation of him, went about with their heads shorn and wore their hair only one finger long. They sheared with stone razors, shaving their hair from the top down and leaving it the length that has been stated. They used stone razors because they had not hit upon the invention of scissors, and they trimmed their hair with great difficulty, as you may well imagine. As a result, when they later saw how easily and delicately the scissors cut, one Inca who was studying reading and writing with us said to my classmate: "If the Spaniards, your forefathers, had done no more than bring us scissors, mirrors, and combs, we would have given them all the gold and silver in our land."[32]

Seeing such relationships may reveal more, ultimately, than watching the novel through the lens of contemporary theorists — Lacan, say, whose emphasis on the significance of mirrors to our development and identity, not to specify his focus on naming, have been implicitly acknowledged by Eltit in confessing to having read him: one of her "sins." The aboriginal repeatedly asserts itself in the novel, not only in such "quotations" but also in the diction — *ruka*: house or hut; *wenumapu*: sky, heaven (where babies come from); *machi*: shaman, healer; *machitú*[n]: healing dance; *toqui*, chieftan; *trutruca*: horn, *quena*: Andean flute, *inche*, I (I am) etc., all these from Mapuche, the Araucanian language still used by the descendants of the once mighty people.[33] By associating the

---

[32] Inca Garcilaso de la Vega, *Comentarios Reales* I, xxii: 39.

[33] Readers interested in rites and diction of the Mapuche Indians, as manifested in Eltit's novel, might consult Ricardo E. Latcham, "Ethnology of the Araucanos," *Journal of the Royal Anthropology Institute* XXXIX (1909): 334-370 and Mischa Titev, *Araucanian Culture in Transition* (Ann Arbor: University of Michigan Press, 1951, especially those sections on "House Types" (23-25) and "The Life Cycle: Birth to Adolescence, Pregnancy Customs" (81-82), and "Curing Rites" (115-117). The latter source is especially illuminating in relation to the ceremonial ending of Section 4, as is

peripheral members of contemporary society with the comparably displaced Indians, both contemporary and ancient, Eltit's allusions enforce a social/historical reading thoroughly backed up by, embodied rather, in her similarly displaced diction.

A way to read the novel, then, and translation proceeds from minutely attentive reading, is by considering any personage, happening, word, or syntax — anything in the novel at all — along the ranges of parallel continua, under the influence of simultaneous coordinates. For examples, we may turn to the range of diction:

arcane/invented: "pritheeing"

↑

spoken: "gutter runnin" ← [*diction*] → written: "trots them in fine style"

↓

current: "entreats"

or to some of the self-avowed repositories of Eltit's literary materials and methods:

James Joyce

↑

El Inca Garcilaso ←   → Jacques Lacan
↓

Carson McCullers

Of course, these schemes are reductive, giving no place, for example, to the little litany of authors in the novel ("Thinks about Lezama Lima . . . James Joyce . . . Neruda Pablo . . . Juan Rulfo . . . E. Pound . . . Robbe Grillet") or to Severo Sarduy, whose novel *Cobra*, she says, "provided a key for entering upon [my] own writing, . . . allowing [me] to think that [my] desires for a certain kind of fiction were realizable";[34] yet so long as we think of the schemes themselves as

---

Sara Castro-Klarén's "Dancing and the Sacred in the Andes: From the Taqui-Oncoy to Rasu-Ñiti," *New World Encounters*, ed. Stephen Greenblatt (Berkeley: University of California Press, 1995), 159-176.

[34] Severo Sarduy, *Cobra*, trans. Suzanne Jill Levine (New York: Dutton, 1975); Elizabeth Burgos, "Palabra Extraviada y Extraviante: Diamela Eltit," *Quimera* 123.194: 21. Sarduy had expressed great admiration for Eltit's work, and she might also have specified Sarduy's *Written on a Body*, trans. Carol Maier (New York: Lumen, 1989) for its precise correspondence to many of

superimposed mutabilities that represent themes and techniques of mutability, we are better tuned to the novel's
Lucretian change, instead of to some Ovidian metamorphosis,
and better focused on the mutability's being *willed* ("she has
sought for herself animal multiformity when she came to
superimposing roaring upon mooing and the neighs"). The
coordinates of this multiformity must be seen as rotary,
replaceable and replacing; any apparently fixed or reliable
coordinate is sooner or later destabilized ("falls"), even though
the end of the book does coincide with a meticulous re-
recapitulation and projects a climax of perception and tran-
scendence ("Her night of glory") such as few modern books
pretend to:

Nothing else occupied her thoughts, until an idea emerged from her
brain: that whole show was for her. She knew with certainty that no
one else at this hour was hanging on that sign's legend, so this
lavishness was meant for her. Someone had mounted this costly
special effect in the city, as a gift for her: with writing and colors,
with colors and motion, engineers' calculations, manual labor,
permits. All this so that she seated in the square at night might truly
let herself be carried away by the blinding light from those glass
tubes which insufflated with colors, powered by batteries, would
subject her to it.

No matter that shortly, with the clearing of dawn, this grand
idea will subside, vanish ("her soul can disappear in this state,
since it was an invention that was offered to each dawn"); that
there is no more "truth" to E. Luminata's projection onto the
sign or in its plunging at her than there is in the ingenious
wizards who bid Don Quixote to battle, only then to despoil
him of his ingeniously begotten heroics. (*Don Quixote*, that
paradigm of the binocular gaze compounded, as with the Duke
and the Duchess in the Part II [here,"Two mountings: the rider
himself and the other who aims at her with the camera"], that
pairing of exalted imagination and a downed-to-earth, a near
lumpen sense, that paternity of all novels, shadows this book
as it does almost all fiction in Spanish and Spanish American.)

---

her tactics and themes. In its Spanish original as well as in its English
translation, Sarduy's collection precedes Jeanette Winterson's novel of similar
title, *Written on the Body*, while both books participate in a *topos* of our
century, joined by Eltit's narrative — all under the evident paternity of
Kafka's "The Penal Colony."

The quiet of the concluding prose as the square ironically comes abuzz with morning's sounds in fact confirms the acute dynamics of the entire work.

Leading to this formal resolution, the varied sections are not helterskelter. They are disparate in their styles, yes; but there are congruences among them, and Eltit has ordered them to near classical dynamic effect. The ten sections might be tentatively labelled this way:

1. Three Cinematic Scenes
2. Interrogation I / Fall of E. Luminata
3. Her Multiform Animal State
4. Images of the Protagonist: Patient/Victim, Reviewing, Second Litany, Indian Rite
5. Self-love / Writing + Printing
6. Proclamations of the City
7. Interrogation II
8. Rehearsing the Cut
9. Performance
10. Epiphany

A dynamic pattern may be glimpsed from even such provisional labels: Sections 1 and 10 frame the work, "retelling" the same narrative of the woman in the square: the first heightened in the images and attitudes presented, the second flattened and more "literal," though containing the climactic perception that leads directly to the dénouement of day's return ("the start of a new cycle"). Between them, Sections 2 and 7 mirror each other in method and manner, as well as in timbre: another literalness, one that is official, documentary, so that even the typeface changes to represent this down-to-business facelessness. Between those two sections, in turn, Section 4 culminates, after a soulful litany of self-Sapphic desire, in a spasmodic crescendo of animality, sexuality, and primitive rite, partly protrayed in vulgar accents, where the language itself celebrates, dances on the page. This first-third climax is matched and surpassed by the end of Section 9, where the novel's themes, motifs, and phrases convulse in a nighttown of rhyme, inversion, spastic meter — a verbal, bovine bacchanal ("vac/a-nal") that in turn gives way to a tranquility in prose nearly the equal of E. Luminata's gray wool dress in which she achieves her triumphal realization by gazing *back* — all this was for *her* — before she sinks into the deafening anonymity of daybreak.

Not only is there a plot to the book, then, there is also a plot to the plotting. For all its fragmentedness, its jagged dis- and re-membering and its looping flicker, the novel obeys a plan that distributes effects and forms with nearly geometrical precision. The book has a structure that belies all suspicion of anything-goes; it is an expressive structure also tending toward baroque exhaustion of material and method in order to conclude, like its protagonist, in almost classic repose.

For the translator, the intransigent ductility of Eltit's diction, the mutability of her line and subject mean constant bending too, ranging from artful dodging of grammatical expectations to impossible — one hears the judgment before-hand — ruses of imitation and substitution. At your back you always hear: get thee to a thesarus and dictionary: *infula* (literal and figurative), *per piacere, combinatorial* (sense 2); to a reform grammar school: "the grass fattens her all's set what weight? what fat?" But following in Eltit's steps, a language away, leads one on a true pilgrimage of her page, ruled, like that other square, where the crossing footsteps are pathways of her words. Góngora again:

> *Pasos de un peregrino son errante*
> *cuantos me dictó versos dulce musa*
> > *en soledad confusa*
> *perdidos unos, otros inspirados*

> (As many as a Pilgrim's errant steps are
> all the verses you sang to me, sweet muse:
> > in a perplexed solitude
> some strayed away, others inspired.)[35]

Errant itself transports two senses, at least, as do the errata of that *straying away*, and Eltit's book reclaims one, vindicates the other — in time, traditions, laws, and life. Her translator ought, at least, to err the like, if he cannot the same.

Trying to err purposefully in the hazardous comple-ment, I realized after six months or so that I would need co-participants, and I gathered what I then called the Translation Posse, till some thorns of that metaphor pricked. Still, the effort often felt like rounding up a wily, elusive work I had

---

[35] Góngora, "[Dedicatoria] al duque de Béjar," Soledades, 37: 1-4.

fallen in love with, at first glance — just one page read — at the first Latin American Book Fair in New York. Impulsively I had written Eltit and her publisher for permission to translate it and begun; to this day most any of its lines prickle my imagination, and the unending translation is still a labor's love. But help was necessary, and I turned to three friends: Gene Bell-Villada, whose collegial generosity and whose active as well as profound knowledge of the language and its literature have often come to my aid; Helen Lane, whose prized translations and long editorial experience, as well as our past exchange of sample translations, guaranteed her value as critical adviser; and Catalina Parra, whose knowledge of Chileanisms, her first-hand experience of the country during the period in which Eltit wrote the novel, and her radical participation in the unofficial art scene during the military dictatorship made her the best of informants. These three collaborators gave me many things, none more precious than the incalculable gift of words and grammars; without these three, I could never have brought my translation to this state of completion, even though I sometimes worked against if not in spite of their recommendations. Criticism yoked to practical suggestion at a global as well as a local level cannot be over appreciated, even when ultimately rejected, forming, as it does, the best basis for articulating the translator's principles. So: I have rejected some of my collaborators' most beautiful solutions because they did not accord with the work's overall fabric as I touch it ("Rejected any solution by beauty").

Despite the biblical tradition, there is a bias against translation undertaken collaboratively. Yet all translation is high collaboration of one sort or another, whether between author and translator, translator and translator, or translator and that wrongfully ignored figure, the editor — not to mention the I and the me, the translator's self-same writer and reader, himself. I did not farm out any of the text — a practice at the root of the bias? —, instead submitting a draft to my colleagues, revised after each of their readings; on occasion I would consult an earlier reader again, but I never brought them together, never showed the readings, save my own, to the others. Neither sheriff nor foreman but frequently referee and director while aiming at being the author's auteur in English, many times I played the magpie; for gather and pick I did, from almost anyone who would suffer questions. Translators and people with an interest in translation tend to be generous in its regard, I find, so I take pride in thanking among such: Sara Castro-Klarén (the first person to render a portion of the novel into English—heroically and admirably), Juan Dávila, Dennis Dollens, Djelal Kadir, María Ester Martínez, Bob Neustadt, Julio Ortega, Irene Rostagno, Raúl Zurita, and both Marjorie Agosín and Juan Carlos Lértora, who examined parts closely; but most especially I thank Jean Franco, Carol Maier, and Francisco Olivero, who reviewed sections and let me put queries to them, as well as William Vesterman, gallant volunteer in editing among all these willing recruits, and consubstatial contributor. Diamela Eltit herself patiently supplied more answers and explanations than could have been necessary to her book's original writing, in turn consulting with the poet Eugenia Brito and Lita Riesenberg, whose contributions cleared many a hurdle for me, thus bringing the circle of collaboration into full linguistic square. (A circle overlapped by the always heartening though, to me, chiefly inapplicable example of Florence Olivier and Anne de Waele's translation of the novel into French [Paris: Des femmes, 1993]. Regrettably I did not have the encouraging example of Everett Fox's inspiriting translation *The Five Books of Moses* [New York: Schocken, 1995].) Finally, I'm pleased to acknowledge Cris Hollingsworth's research, which rescued me, and Zed and Lily Cannon's tigerish tenacity in eying, from every possible angle, all my work. Much of which would never have been possible without funds and understanding — the *time* — provided by grants from Rutgers University, the National Endowment for the Arts, and the New York State Council on the Arts.

The result of all this consultation, editing, interpretation and counter-interpretation may open to you a work formidable in its essence, essential in its method; a book inescapably ours — all of us — in its subject and treatment, while still loyal to a promise of Latin American literature to speak its own language, languages, in its own ways, about its own themes, and to speak them bold out into the whole world. Eltit's novel never flinches; you will, I think, as I unquestionably have, in recognizing what it brings forth in us, our language, and our literature; and then you may renew the attack. At those moments, and many others in these pages, in the course of the whole work, you may know again that rare gratification of a writer's courage basking in the satisfaction of a reader's bravery.

Ronald Christ
Santa Fe, 1997

DATE DUE

Lumen and SITES Books

The Narrow Act: Borges' Art of Allusion
Ronald Christ
ISBN: 0-930829-34-4. $15.00

Written on a Body
Severo Sarduy
Translated by Carol Maier
ISBN: 0-930829-04-2. $8.95

Borges in/and/on Film
Edgardo Cozarinsky
Translated by Gloria Waldman & Ronald Christ
ISBN: 0-930829-08-5. $10.95

Space in Motion
Juan Goytisolo
Translated by Helen Lane
ISBN: 0-930829-03-4. $9.95

Reverse Thunder, A Dramatic Poem
Diane Ackerman
ISBN: 0-930829-09-3. $7.95

Dialogue in the Void: Beckett & Giacometti
Matti Megged
ISBN: 0-930829-01-8. $7.95

The Animal That Never Was: In Search of the Unicorn
Matti Megged
ISBN: 0-930829-20-4. $12.95

Byron and the Spoiler's Art
Paul West
ISBN: 0-930829-13-1. $12.95

Urban Voodoo
Edgardo Cozarinsky
ISBN: 0-930829-15-8. $9.95

Under a Mantle of Stars
Manuel Puig
Translated by Ronald Christ
ISBN: 0-930829-00-X. $10.00

Refractions
Octavio Armand
Translated by Carol Maier
ISBN: 0-930829-21-2. $15.00

Lumen and SITES Books
www.sitesarch.org

ZenLux: Architecture & Electronics
Duncan Brown
ISBN: 0-930829-39-5. $15.00

Deconstructing the Kimbell:
An Essay on Meaning and Architecture
Michael Benedikt
ISBN: 0-930829-16-6. $15.95

For an Architecture of Reality
Michael Benedikt
ISBN: 0-930829-05-0. $10.95

The Architecture of Enric Miralles & Carme Pinos
Peter Buchanan, Dennis Dollens,
Josep Maria Montaner, Lauren Kogod
ISBN: 0-930829-14-X. $20.0

Independent Projects: Experimental Architecture,
Design + Research in New York
Anne Van Ingen & Dennis Dollens
ISBN: 0-930829-18-2. $20.00

SITES Architecture 26
ISBN: 0-930829-33-6. $20.00

Josep Maria Jujol: Five Major Buildings 1913-1923
Dennis Dollens
ISBN: 0-930829-35-2. $20.00

The Architecture of Jujol
Josep Maria Jujol, Jr.
Translated, Edited, & Introduced by Ronald Christ
0-930829-38-7. $25.00

LAX: The Los Angeles Experiment
Mick McConnell
ISBN: 0-930829-36-0. $25.00

Trade and library orders to:
Consortium Book Sales and Distrubution
800-283-3572